SERGEI

A VERY RUSSIAN ROMANCE

Victoria Wright

Universal Romance
United States of America

For more information, please visit:

www.universalromance.com

Publisher's Note: This is a work of fiction. Names, characters, places, and incidents are a product of the author's imagination. Locales and public names are sometimes used for atmospheric purposes. Any resemblance to actual people, living or dead, or to businesses, companies, events, institutions, or locales is completely coincidental.

Printed in the United States of America

Sergei / Victoria Wright. -- 2nd ed.
ISBN 9781519085641

Contents

CHAPTER I

Moscow

Eleanor had never been the best at keeping secrets but there was no way in hell she was about to tell her mother that she'd been called to Moscow to help investigate a serial killer. It just wasn't going to happen. Especially not after she'd spent six days telling said mother not to worry about anything.

"Are you sure it's safe? You know, over there?" her mother had asked when she called a week earlier. Eleanor called her as soon as she was asked to go, because there was also no way she was going to take her six-year-old daughter on the trip. To start with, Ana didn't even have a passport.

"Yes Mom, I swear it's safe," she'd promised, making an effort to sound as reassuring as possible instead of slightly-exasperated like she really felt. "It's the capital of the country, I'll be in a hotel like a mile from the Kremlin. I'll probably be able to see the FSB headquarters from my window."

"Is that a good thing? What's the FSV?" her mother asked.

"The FSB, Mom. It's the state security agency, like the FBI. Look, just don't worry about it okay? I promise everything will be fine. I just need you to look after Ana for two weeks while I'm gone. Can you do that for me?"

"Of course, I already agreed to take her, but don't I have a right to be concerned about my only daughter?" she persisted. "You know I'm not totally ignorant of the news, I know it's not all sunshine and roses in that part of the world."

"But it's not all doom and gloom either, Mom," Eleanor pointed out. "And we're talking about a business trip. It's just two weeks, I'll be there and back before you know it. I just need you to spend some time with the granddaughter you adore so much."

"You know I love her every bit as much as I loved you," her mother replied. "Do you think you'll find her father while you're there?"

Eleanor couldn't help but to roll her eyes.

"Mom, it's the largest country on the planet."

"So? You're going to the capital!"

"So there's like a hundred-and-fifty million people in the country, and I promise you they don't all live in Moscow."

"Why not? If I lived in Russia, that's where I'd want to be..." her mother insisted.

"Of course you would, Mom. It's one of the most expensive cities in the world to live in. But that's all beside the point; it's not where he lives."

"How do you know?" she asked.

"Because he never mentioned it," she sighed. There were a lot of things Ana's father had never mentioned. "He talked about a village. Kayuga or something, I don't know. It definitely wasn't Moscow, though. Besides, I'm pretty sure there are a million men named Sergei in Russia."

"Well it couldn't hurt to ask," she pressed.

"Okay, please stop. I didn't call to talk about going on some wild goose chase in Russia. I called because I need to go on a business trip," Eleanor said, attempting to redirect their conversation.

"Who ever said anything about a wild goose chase?" her mother asked. "I just thought if you're going there anyway, why not try to find the father of your child while you're at it? But it's just a thought, that's all."

"You're going to drive me insane with this," Eleanor sighed. "Alright, moving on now. I'll bring Ana over on Saturday if that works for you."

"You said your flight is on Sunday afternoon?" her mother asked, finally letting the topic drop.

"Yes."

"Better to drop her off on Friday then," she said. "It'll give you more time to put everything in order."

So it was that with a feeling of mixed relief Eleanor made her preparations that week, dropped her daughter off with a kiss on Friday afternoon, and found herself seated on board flight AF1763 from Seattle to the Charles de Gaulle International Airport and then onward to Russia. It wasn't the first time she'd flown, but there was something different about the experience this time and it wasn't just the fact she was flying internationally. Despite everything she'd said to her mother, there was a small part of her that hoped beyond hope for the impossible to happen. It made her stomach flip in anxious anticipation even as her heart ached from the memories and her knees jittered all the way from Paris to Moscow.

When the plane finally touched down and she felt the tires skidding over the tarmac, a preternatural calm came over her. Sitting back in her seat, she waited for the plane to reach its terminal, and then, grateful for her window seat, kept waiting as her fellow passengers hustled and bustled past one another, each one of them more eager than the next to disembark.

As the final passengers inched down the narrow aisle, Eleanor stood and stretched her sore muscles. The second leg of her flight, from Paris to Moscow, hadn't been nearly as long as the flight from Seattle but three-and-a-half hours was still a long time to spend sitting in the same position and her back cracked audibly as she stretched. Grabbing her carry-on bag, she followed the last of the passengers down the aisle and into the arrivals area.

It was crowded with people from at least three different flights, and with only nine desks functioning she figured it was going to be a while. Finding an empty seat that was as out of the way as she could get, she settled in to wait for a lull in the lines. It gave her an opportunity to look around and observe her fellow travelers. Many of them were from the same Seattle flight that she'd taken out of the States, including a family with three young kids that looked as tired as Eleanor felt, but they were far outnumbered by European nationals and native Russians returning to the country.

Pushing her laptop bag under the chair, she leaned back and let her head rest against the wall behind her, allowing her heavy eyelids to drift shut. As soon as she did, images from the past leapt to the forefront of her mind. Pitch black ink that took the form of an imperial, double-headed eagle with its wingtips stretched from shoulder to well-muscled shoulder–she'd been mesmerized by it the first time she saw him shirtless.

Sergei. From the moment they'd met, she knew her life would never be the same. Her heart constricted at the memory, a tight and unpleasant feeling in the center of her chest, but she focused on breathing and it eased away. It hadn't always been so easy to deal with; she could still vividly remember the kind of pain that'd left her doubled over in agony and on the way to the ER more than once. Whoever knew heartbreak could hurt so much?

"Ms. Truman?" a lightly-accented voice interrupted her reminiscing.

Eleanor's head snapped up, bleary eyes opening to stare at the person standing in front of her. "Yes?"

"Are you Ms. Eleanor Truman?" the woman asked again, glancing between Eleanor and a picture in her hand. "Could I see your passport, *pozhaluysta?*"

It took her a few moments of fumbling through her pockets before Eleanor remembered having tucked her passport into the outer pocket of her laptop bag. Fishing it out, she passed it to the woman with an apologetic look.

"Is there a problem?" she asked.

"*Nyet,* no problem," the woman answered as she flipped open Eleanor's passport to confirm her identity. "Mr. Kossakov asked me to meet you and take you to the hotel. I am Nadya Stepanova, so if you'll just come with me we'll get your documents stamped and be on our way."

Mr. Kossakov was the Russian investigator who had contacted her office to request her assistance on a case he'd been working for some time. She didn't know the full details yet, but it involved the deaths of at least nine people. When he went looking for a criminal psychologist to consult with, her name wound up on the shortlist and she was the one willing to travel abroad in order to hear more about the case and give a professional opinion.

Grabbing her laptop bag, Eleanor followed the slender woman. As haggard as she felt, her gaze still moved up naturally to scan over the crowd as some foolish ray of hope inspired her to search for Sergei amidst the sea of unfamiliar faces. It was impossible though, and her eyes fell to the back of Nadya's head and her hair, expertly swept up into a neat bun.

Ten minutes, another passport stamp, and three inspections later, Nadya led the way to baggage claim and they waited another twenty minutes to collect Eleanor's luggage. It was twenty minutes that usually would have been very awkward, but Eleanor was so exhausted that she no longer cared. In fact, she actually took the initiative and started a conversation.

"Have you worked with Mr. Kossakov long?" she asked.

"Yes," Nadya responded, smiling. "Since I was nineteen."

"Ah, so I guess it's been a while," she said. "Is he nice?"

"He is a good friend of my father," Nadya explained. "I've worked for him thirteen years now, it's always been very good. He's very fond of foreigners, so I'm sure you'll like him."

"I've always heard that Russians were very hospitable to their guests, but I had no idea Mr. Kossakov would send someone to the airport. Thank you for going to all the trouble," she said.

"Oh it's not a problem," Nadya assured her. "In Russia we always make sure to take good care of our guests. You could say it is like a national tradition we have. And trust me, if I didn't come to get you, it would have taken you hours to get through that mess."

"Well I certainly appreciate it. To tell you the truth, I can't wait to get some rest. This is the longest flight I've ever been on," Eleanor confessed with a yawn, covering her mouth with the back of her hand. It was hard to stay standing, and she felt like someone had placed leaden weights on her eyelids.

Fortunately, it wasn't long before the baggage carousel began to move and after a few minutes of watching other people's luggage fill up the conveyer belt Eleanor spotted the first of her two bags, a smaller duffel bag. Her second, larger suitcase, followed soon after and Nadya led the way to a waiting car.

Once seated and buckled in the car, Eleanor let her head rest against the window, grateful for the cool glass against her temple. She must have dozed off because the next thing she knew, they'd arrived at the hotel and Nadya politely nudged her awake. A porter helped them unload her luggage, and Nadya handled the front desk with ease that spoke to previous experience. Before she knew it, Eleanor found herself whisked up an elevator to the fourth floor of the Aurora Royale and escorted to her suite. The porter left her bags in the middle of the room for her, took his tip from Nadya, and closed the door as he left.

"This will be your suite for the duration of your stay. The hotel has two pools and an on-site spa, a cocktail bar, and a restaurant. Clearly you're very tired," Nadya observed with a smile. "So I will leave you to get some rest. It's just past six o'clock now. They will bring you a fresh, hot meal in fifteen minutes. I strongly advise you to eat before you sleep. Tomorrow, Mr. Kossakov will come to meet you at two o'clock for lunch; I've left a note on the back of this card."

"That sounds perfect," she said with a sigh of relief. The thought of sleep hadn't been so inviting since her first months as a new mother, when Ana's restlessness and fits of crying kept her up through the night for weeks on end. She couldn't wait to fall into the plush bed.

"Here are your card keys, they also let you into the pool," Nadya said, setting the plastic cards down on the small desk.

"I don't think I'll be using the pool, but I'll keep that in mind. Thank you so much Nadya, I trust we'll see each other again while I'm here?"

"I'm certain of it," Nadya agreed. "Have a good night."

With that, she turned and left the room, closing the door quietly as she exited. Alone in the suite, Eleanor stepped through the open door into the bedroom and sank onto the edge of the bed, overcome by a feeling of total exhaustion. It'd been approximately twenty-six hours since she slept, not counting a brief nap on the layover in Paris. She barely had the energy to remove her shoes, and that task must have taken longer than she thought because soon there was a knock on her door and room service had arrived.

Nadya, or perhaps Mr. Kossakov, had arranged for a meal of hot borscht, meat-filled Russian dumplings, roasted potatoes smothered in sour cream, and the fluffiest bread she'd eaten in years. It was all perfectly prepared and perfectly delicious, complimented by a savory red wine and ice cold water with a twist of lemon. One meal fit for a queen (or perhaps a tsarina?) and the briefest of showers later, she slipped into the pillow-soft confines of the bed and soon fell fast asleep.

CHAPTER II

Kossakov

It was almost ten when Eleanor awoke the next morning. After taking a more relaxing shower and washing her hair, she unloaded her suitcase and got dressed.

Since she was on a business trip, she'd packed light, bringing with her only the bare necessities for her stay. That included her toiletries, three pairs of pajamas, and ten days worth of clean clothes so she had plenty of time to locate the hotel laundry room.

Of course, on top of that she had her phone, her tablet, and her laptop. None of which she'd bothered to hook up to the hotel WiFi the night before, so she made a quick call for room service and promptly set about getting online. No sooner had she connected to the WiFi then her email began dinging her with new messages. Spam, spam, and more spam, followed by an email from her mother with pictures of Ana attached.

'I'm sure you're probably asleep at the hotel by now, but send me a message when you get up in the morning. We'll be waiting. Lots of love, - Mom & Ana'

A quick mental conversion told her it was midnight in Washington, so Eleanor set her phone aside and typed up a short response to her mother. Room service arrived a few minutes later with a knock at the door, delivering a carafe of hot coffee and a covered platter with her breakfast. The aroma of the coffee roused her appetite, filling the air as she poured her first, steaming cup.

Adding cream and sugar to her taste, she lifted it to her lips and savored the fragrance before taking a sip. Her taste buds weren't disappointed by the explosion of flavor that burst across her tongue; it was hard to imagine a more delightful way to start the morning. And what a beautiful morning it was. Crossing her suite to the window, she parted the heavy outer curtains to allow more sunlight into the room, peeking through the sheer, white privacy curtains to get her first real look at Russia.

It was early June, the beginning of summer in Moscow, and every tree was heavily leafed with dense, green foliage. Cracking her window open, she was greeted by a breeze of cool, fresh air. It must have rained sometime during the night or early morning, Eleanor could smell it in the air. There was something wonderfully different about the smell of Russia compared to her hometown in Washington, it made her feel refreshed and invigorated.

Perhaps unsurprisingly, it also reminded her of Sergei. How many nights had she spent in his arms, listening to the sound of his voice as he regaled her with tales from his youth and promised that they would return to his homeland together? So much for all of that.

The thought sent a lance of pain through her chest, but it wasn't the passionately raw, burning sort of pain from years past. Rather, it was the dull, aching pain of a heart hardened by time and the reluctant acceptance of what seemed to her an inexplicably cruel fate.

Turning away from her window with a sigh, she settled back at the small table to eat her breakfast before it was entirely cold. Like her coffee, the omelette she'd ordered was magnificent, a light, fluffy creation perfectly imbued with sautéed onions, shredded spinach, thinly-sliced mushrooms, and topped with a layer of grated cheese. Adding salt and pepper to taste, she tucked in and was soon scraping the plate clean with the edge of her fork.

With nothing else to do for another two-and-a-half hours, she tidied up around the bed and then donned her shoes and a light jacket to head out. She'd known that coming to Russia was sure to bring up all sorts of memories, but she was determined that a ghost from her past was not going to ruin her present and future enjoyment of life. Not anymore than he already had, anyway.

So, tucking her passport safely into her deepest pocket, she tossed her room key, cellphone, and wallet into her purse and made her way down to the lobby. It was quiet downstairs, with just a handful of people milling about and a single clerk behind the main desk who was presently checking in an elderly gentleman and his wife.

Once outside, she paused to orient herself, glancing up and down the street and taking a long look at the entry of her hotel. The last thing she needed was to forget what her building looked like or get lost on her first day in the country.

Feeling reasonably confident that she would be able to find her way back unassisted, Eleanor set off in the direction of what Google Maps assured her was a public park. She'd spent two days staring at the streets in an attempt to familiarize herself with the area, but it still took her half an hour of passing boutique shops and high-end restaurants to find the park. Just as she prepared to turn back, Eleanor spied the entrance of the Moscow Hermitage Gardens.

"About time," she sighed under her breath. Why did things always look so much closer together on the map?

The expedition was worth it, though. Despite the fact that there were throngs of people present and she'd never much enjoyed crowds, she made her way through the gardens.

It was warmer than she'd anticipated, so she soon removed her jacket to better enjoy the intermittent breeze. In the garden, young couples walked hand-in-hand or relaxed together in the shade as children ran and played on a small playground, their enthusiastic shrieks filling the air. On a bench near the playground sat a neat little row of old ladies, babushkas presumably, chatting amidst themselves as they kept watch over the children.

Eleanor felt a strange surge of warmth at the sight, and would have liked to join the women in conversation, to ask them about their grandchildren or their lives in Russia, but she'd only picked up a handful of words from Sergei before he vanished from her life.

So she lingered for a while, enjoying the sunshine and flowers, and watching the other visitors. Soon it was time to return to the hotel for her meeting with Kossakov, but as she turned away from the playground and the council of watchful babushkas, she heard a woman calling out.

"Seryozha, idi syuda!"

For a moment her breath froze in her lungs and her heart skipped a beat. Unable to stop herself, she turned back to glance in the woman's direction, just in time to see a young boy leave the playground and run headlong toward her. Against her will, Eleanor felt her heart sink in disappointment as the mother and child embraced.

Of course it isn't him, she chastised herself as she returned to the hotel. *What was this mindless hope that refused to die?* Sergei had gone, left her without a note or trace, and after what she'd learned in the years since then she had to assume he was dead. If he wasn't, and they ever crossed paths again, she might just do the honors herself.

It was fifteen minutes until two o'clock when she got back to the hotel, just enough time to return to her room and prepare for Mr. Kossakov's arrival. Unsure quite what to expect, she decided to pack her slender, traveling tech bag with her laptop and tablet.

Dropping her phone into its dedicated pocket, she transferred the room key to the same pocket as her passport, and tucked her wallet into an inner, zippered pouch in the bag. She'd never been much for make-up to begin with, but after Ana's birth the last of her lingering acne seemed to have cleared up for good so she'd tossed everything except mascara and never looked back. Applying a dash to her upper eyelashes, she checked her overall appearance one last time in the bathroom mirror and then settled on the edge of the bed to wait.

At a minute past two, the phone rang and she rushed to answer it.

"Ms. Truman," the clerk at the front desk greeted her. "Mr. Kossakov has arrived for your lunch, please meet him in the lobby."

"Thank you, please tell him I'm on my way," she answered. Placing the phone back in its cradle, she grabbed her bag and went to meet the investigator who'd called on her for help from halfway around the world.

Mr. Kossakov, as it turned out, was every bit as friendly and genial as Nadya had said he was. He was the only one sitting in the lobby when she came down, a slightly heavyset man in his early fifties. His hair was dark, though streaked through with strands of gray and white, and he sported a full, impressive beard. He was also impeccably dressed, wearing a navy blue, fitted suit that was so dark it looked almost black until the light hit it, with a pristine white shirt.

"Ms. Truman," he greeted her with a broad smile, standing as she approached and extending his hand to her. "I am Mikhail Kossakov. Thank you for coming all this way to meet me."

"Of course," Eleanor said, shaking his hand warmly. "I admit your request came rather out of the blue, but I'm always happy to help where I can. I should be the one to thank you for taking care of all the preparations."

"*Konechno*," Kossakov said, waving a hand dismissively. "It's the least I can do after asking you to come so far from home, and on short notice too. And now, I'm sure you must be eager to learn more about why I called you here."

"To say the least," Eleanor agreed.

The only thing she knew so far was that he needed help profiling a serial killer; aside from that, he'd kept her in the dark and a fairly exhaustive internet search failed to bring up any cases that seemed to match Kossakov's limited description. She had, for all intents and purposes, accepted the assignment blind.

It was out of character for her–usually she required a detailed case file with all known, pertinent facts at hand, before agreeing to take on a project. But Kossakov's request piqued her interest, and Russia, as much as Kossakov's mysterious case, seemed to be calling to her.

With Kossakov leading, they made their way to the restaurant just off the hotel lobby, and were soon seated at a quiet table near the front windows. The investigator had brought his own bag with him, and once they'd placed an order for drinks and appetizers he unzipped it to withdraw a thick binder.

"This is what I have compiled to date," he explained, setting the binder on the table between them. "They are copies, for you. I have translated the most important parts first since you don't understand Russian very well."

"Alright, so what exactly are we looking at here?" she asked. "You said you're reasonably sure you have a serial killer on your hands. What are the facts?"

It was strange to think that Sergei was the reason she was finally there, in Russia, even though he was long gone. Up until her relationship with him, Eleanor had felt adrift in life, able to subsist but uncertain what more to do with her existence.

Everything changed after him, and not just because of Ana. Once they were apart, she'd become determined to unravel the secrets he'd kept from her; secrets about himself that'd been hidden in plain sight, encoded into the very tattoos that adorned his body. Sometimes she wondered, if she'd known from the start what that dark ink entailed, would everything still have happened the same?

Probably.

As it was, once she learned what the tattoos meant, pursuing a degree in criminal psychology seemed only natural. What better way was there to understand her vanished lover?

In any case, it was the method she had available to her, and she seized it. Turned out, she was pretty good at it too. By the time she finished her field training and graduated, she'd received over a dozen offers of employment.

"We are more than reasonably sure," Kossakov corrected, breaking her out of her thoughts. "There is no shadow of a doubt. I did not wish to alarm you before you arrived, but this is a serious case. There have already been nine murders, and we believe there will be more."

CHAPTER III

Nightfall

Nine murders, executed with identical precision, at nine separate locations in the greater Moscow and St. Petersburg areas. Eleanor hadn't even looked at half the contents of the file that Kossakov left with her, but she was certain she'd never encountered such a gruesome case before. The Russian investigator was right, if the killer was still loose there would undoubtedly be more deaths.

After a lunch consisting of more borscht topped with sour cream and fresh dill, beef stroganoff with tender egg noodles, and rye bread with caviar (a strange yet not unpleasant combination), Kossakov had talked her through the highlights of the file and they'd agreed to meet again the day after next. It was late evening when Eleanor decided she'd had enough of looking through crime-scene photos and autopsy reports for the day. The sun had set and the sky over Moscow was finally going dark, losing the last remnants of light from the vanished sun. Soon only the artificial light of the city would be left to illuminate the darkness.

The window in her room afforded her a good view of the street below, still busy and thronging with people despite the increasingly late hour. The boutique shops had closed for the night, but their storefronts remained lit for the enjoyment of passersby, and the restaurants that had entertained a mellow atmosphere during the day were alive with activity. Traffic continued moving on the street, but the noise of squealing brakes, revving engines, honking horns, and the not-uncommon battle of swearing hurled between irate motorists was softened almost into silence by the double-paned glass.

Half-past ten in Moscow meant it was just past noon in Washington. Stepping away from the window, she retrieved her phone from where it'd been charging on the table. Calling home would be slightly expensive with roaming charges but it was worth it to say hello and hear her daughter's voice. After three rings her mother answered.

"Eleanor," she greeted her. "It's about time, what took you so long to call?"

"It hasn't been that long," Eleanor defended. "And besides, I did send an email. It was just a long day. Anyway, hello to you too, and thanks for the pictures."

"Did you meet the Russian?" she asked next.

"Yes mom, I had lunch with Mr. Kossakov today," she confirmed.

"And? What was he like? How did it go?" Her mother had a unique way of bombarding her with an endless barrage of questions, and this was no exception.

"It was a perfectly standard business meeting. So far he's been very polite, and he has a very nice assistant named Nadya who met me at the airport and got me through customs in no time," Eleanor said, settling comfortably on the small couch as she spoke. "How's Ana doing?"

"Oh she's fine, just finishing her macaroni right now. I'll put her on once she's washed her hands," her mother answered. "So how was the flight? What do you think of Moscow?"

"I think I haven't had a chance to see much of the city yet, so I'm not sure," she sighed. "There are some seriously beautiful buildings along this street though, and they've got almost as many trees as we do. It's... pretty. And the food is incredible so far; I've had borscht, some kind of meat-stuffed dumplings, little fruit-filled pastries, and the best stroganoff ever."

"That's good, how's the weather? Did you take your warm jacket like I told you to?"

"The weather is fine," Eleanor replied, certain her mother could hear the rolling of her eyes in the tone of her voice. "Just like I knew it would be, because a little something called the internet told me. So no, I did not pack the jacket that takes up a third of my suitcase, but all the same I'm relatively sure I won't freeze to death."

"Oh don't get sassy with me now, you wouldn't even be there if it wasn't for me," her mother warned defensively. "And besides, you never know. It is Russia, they're a very northern nation."

"Mom, it's the middle of summer," she groaned, wishing she could knock her head against the wall.

"So?" she challenged. "You know very well this global warming thing is making the whole planet's weather crazy, I heard they had hail the size of golf balls a few years ago."

"That was Chicago," Eleanor informed her. "But look, I don't wanna argue about it. I promise I'll buy a coat at the first sign of an incoming blizzard, okay?"

"That's fine, dear. Just do what you think is best," she answered. "Oh, Ana's just finished up. Hold on, I'll help her wash up and put her on the phone."

Eleanor sighed, shaking her head as her mother put the phone down and stepped away. She meant well, but lord the woman drove her positively nuts sometimes.

"Mama! Finally, I've been waiting for you. Did you get the pictures Grandma sent?" Ana greeted her boisterously a few minutes later, and Eleanor instantly forgot her mild frustration with her own mother's antics.

"I sure did, sweetheart, you're just as cute as ever. Are you being good for Grandma?" she asked.

"Yes, and after dinner I helped wash the dishes," Ana answered. "Uh, how long will you be gone? 'Cause I really miss you, Mama."

"Just about two weeks," Eleanor said. "It's just a short business trip, and then I'll be back. Don't worry, Grandma will make sure you have lots of fun while I'm gone. You won't even notice how fast time passes."

"Will you call every day?" she asked. Her already-childish voice sounded extra small and concerned, and it tugged sharply at Eleanor's heartstrings. What had she been thinking to go on a two week business trip on such short notice?

"I'll try, baby bear," she answered, suddenly feeling immensely guilty for leaving so abruptly. Although Ana had spent the weekend with her grandmother several times before, two weeks must have seemed like an eternity to the mind of a six-year-old.

"Okay, and Mama?" Ana continued questioningly.

"Yes?"

"Don't forget to bring me lots of pictures," the little girl instructed, bringing a broad smile to Eleanor's face.

"Of course," she promised. "I'll bring you back lots of presents, too. Just be as good as you always are, and I'll try to call at least every other day. Remember, Mama's got a lot of work to do while I'm here, and there's a big, big time difference between us. Like right now, I bet the sun is shining for you."

"It is," Ana confirmed.

"But guess what?" Eleanor said. "Here it's nighttime, and I can see the moon."

"Really?" she asked.

"You better believe it," Eleanor answered. "And tonight when you see the moon, I'll be looking at the sun again. So don't worry, I'll call as often as I can and you can have grandma send me any pictures you want."

"Okay Mama," Ana said. "Do your work and come home as fast as you can."

"I will," Eleanor promised. "I love you, my little bear cub. Tell grandma I love her, too."

"Okay, love you too!" Ana proclaimed and a moment later the line went dead. Eleanor set her phone aside with a smile and a shake of her head. Yawning widely, she covered the back of her mouth and stood to stretch before shuffling toward the bed. After a brief struggle to divest herself of unwanted clothes, she flopped face-down onto the bed and clicked the light off. Exhausted, her mind went blessedly blank, and she slipped away into the sweet oblivion of dreams.

The next day found Eleanor poring over Kossakov's case file again.

Arkady Semenov - Julia Steinbeck - Vadim Berzinsky - Tula Lemonova - Valeriy Vodovsky - Natasha Cherkova - Artyom Alekseev - Olga Titova - Nikita Sokolov

Five men and four women, ranging in age from a tender seventeen to sixty-one years old. The killer targeted natives and foreigners with no apparent distinction, but he was definitely alternating from male to female and back. Which meant the next body they found would belong to a woman. The thought was enough to send a cold shudder down her spine. Was she still alive, or already dead?

One thing was sure–the killer was no modern Ripper. Far from targeting prostitutes, or even petty criminals, the victims had professions ranging from carpentry and welding to a lawyer, a teacher, a doctor, and a physicist. Blind chance, perhaps, but Eleanor was looking for any possible pattern to the murders. Something motivated the killer to choose those people as victims, she just had to figure out what it was.

From what she could understand of the translated pages and Kossakov's brief, handwritten notations, there hadn't been any taunting messages or notes to the police, no cryptic messages of any kind. And not a single witness, not a single discernible clue to be found at any of the crime scenes, not a footprint, a hair, or one trace of the perpetrator. It was almost as though a ghost had committed the murders and left each body intricately strung up with copper wire for the authorities to find.

There's got to be a common theme. But what was it? The first victim was twenty-five years old, the second thirty-four. Vadim Berzinky was only seventeen, then Tula Lemonova at forty-three years old. Vodovsky was fifty-two, Cherkova twenty-five, and Alekseev forty-four. Titova was thirty-nine, and Sokolov the oldest at sixty-one. Was the killer simply striking at random, an opportunist with a thirst for blood? It would have explained the fact that each body was found at a different location, strung up identically from a tree.

Looking at the crime scene photos, Eleanor seriously doubted the killings were random. Perhaps the victims didn't have any connection to each other, but the killer chose each one for a reason.

CHAPTER IV

Sergei

Nadya arrived early the next afternoon to take her to Kossakov's office. It was a forty minute drive from the hotel, mostly because the roads in between were choked with the traffic of angry motorists. Fortunately, Nadya handled the drive like only a seasoned native could, shifting between lanes, cornering, and swinging in and out of tight positions with ease. Watching her drive through, Eleanor was immensely grateful she didn't have to navigate the mess of Moscow's city streets; she wasn't sure she would've been able to handle it without getting into an accident, let alone with the same serene grace that Nadya maintained.

"So, do you like Moscow so far?" Nadya asked as they waited at a red light. At least that much was the same, though several other cars sailed through the intersection anyway, managing to narrowly avoid colliding with cross-traffic.

"So far so good," Eleanor answered with a smile. "I haven't seen much yet, of course, but I did take a walk down to the Hermitage Garden. It's nice to see so many trees, too; it reminds me of my home state."

Except that Washington didn't have any creepy serial killers stringing people up from trees with copper wire. After spending the day before absorbed in the file, she'd been happy to stay in the safe confines of her hotel with a room service dinner–there was no telling what monsters lurked in the shadowed city beyond the lobby doors. A shiver ran down her spine, and she redirected her attention to the streets in an effort to find some distraction from her thoughts.

Their destination was in the southwest of the city, near where the city limits met with a mix of farmland and untamed wilderness. And the further they drove from the city center, with its embassies, hotels, and various tourist accommodations, the more dilapidated things appeared. For the most part, the road was evenly paved and well-maintained, but as she peered past the curtain of trees that lined the streets it was plain to see that most of the buildings were in a state of disrepair. Graffiti was visible on some of the buildings they passed, while others suffered from peeling paint, cracks in the foundation walls, or boarded-up windows. It was a strange sight compared to the many modern, newly-designed buildings stretching out from the city center. There were some newer apartment buildings, and condominiums, built amidst the Soviet-era tenements but they were few and guarded by fences with security gates at the entrances. The vast majority of the residents had installed windows to enclose their balconies, and practically every unit sported an identical air conditioning unit attached to the side of the building.

"Welcome to Rossiya," Nadya said with a throaty laugh when she saw how Eleanor was looking intently at their surroundings. "Is not quite what you expected, no?"

"Oh, I don't know," Eleanor said, her cheeks coloring in embarrassment. She didn't want to come across as a judgmental foreigner, or some fainting lily fresh from her pampered Western life. "I'm not sure what I expected. I've heard it was really hard here, back during the '90s."

"It was a wild time, to be sure," Nadya said, "criminals stole whatever was not nailed down, you could say. Our country has faced many troubles, but we are good at surviving. We have struggled and overcome."

"That's what I've heard," Eleanor said, nodding. Her thoughts were thousands of miles and seven years away though, lost in memories of the one who'd first told her about what Russia was like in the aftermath of the Soviet Union's dissolution. She'd lain in his arms, wrapped in the loving warmth of his embrace and listening intently to every word that fell from his lips. She must have traced each of his tattoos a dozen times with her fingertips, curious but ignorant of their true meaning. He simply shrugged when she asked, telling her they were the marks of a lost youth. And in a minimalist kind of way, he'd told the truth. There was so much he didn't say, though; his silence had haunted her for years.

Their arrival at the building that housed Kossakov's office forced Eleanor out of her thoughts. She followed Nadya, entering through a solid metal door that swung shut heavily behind them. The interior of the building had seen better days, but it was clean, didn't smell, and must have been repainted sometime in the recent past because the walls weren't stained or peeling. A small lift, just big enough for three people to fit without being crammed in like sardines, carried them up to the twelfth floor and Kossakov's office.

"Welcome to my humble office," the investigator greeted her. "Please make yourself comfortable. Would you like some tea or maybe coffee?"

"Thank you, I think I'm fine. The hotel serves an impressive buffet in the morning, so I just helped myself to that," Eleanor said, setting her bag down as she took a seat across the desk from Kossakov.

Humble was a polite term for his office. It consisted of a small outer room with two chairs, what had to be the world's smallest couch, and a tiny desk with a chair for Nadya. A heavy wooden door separated the entry (to call it a waiting room would be generous indeed) from Kossakov's personal office, so it at least felt more private, but it also felt very small. The office itself was actually of a decent size but there were no windows, and bookcases or filing cabinets laden with various books and documents lined each wall except where the door was. In approximately the center of the room was Kossakov's behemoth of a desk, most of its surface also covered with paperwork or books, and with two chairs in front of it. They were soft, comfortable arm chairs though, so once she sat down Eleanor felt more at ease and the room even seemed a bit less cramped.

"*Khorosho.* Nadya," the Russian called through the open door between them. "*Prinesi chai, pozhaluysta.*"

With his tea on the way, Kossakov got right down to business with Eleanor. They had a killer to catch, and no time to waste.

"So, now is a good time for you to ask questions," he said. "What are your thoughts so far, about the case, and what would you like to know?"

"Well, it's a very disturbing case. I think it's safe to say that the killer is going to strike again, and based on the pattern so far it will be another woman. He's meticulously detail-oriented, and probably observes a strict daily schedule or ritual. At first glance, though, his victims appear to be chosen at random, almost indiscriminately," Eleanor said. "Combined with the total lack of witnesses to any of his crimes, that could indicate that he's an opportunistic killer."

"No, no, this is a good theory but here," he shuffled through the papers on his desk and pulled out a thin folder with three pages. "I did not have a chance to translate this for you, but we have very strong reason to believe the man is purposefully targeting the victims.

"*Spasibo,*" he finished, addressing Nadya as she quietly entered to deliver his steaming cup of tea.

"What's that?" Eleanor asked after the door closed, indicating the document in his hand.

"This is a witness statement provided by my client," Kossakov said, setting it on the table between them. It was written in Cyrillic, in such impossibly-small print that Eleanor doubted she would have been able to read it even if she understood Russian and its strange alphabet.

"I thought there weren't any witnesses," she said.

"This is the only one so far," Kossakov explained, blowing over the surface of his tea before taking a sip. "It was sent to me last week."

"Okay," she regarded the alien text, then glanced back to the investigator. "I take it he's a relative of one of the deceased?"

"She," Kossakov corrected. "*Da,* Oksana is the mother of the last woman that was killed, Olga Titova. She's an old woman now so her son initiated the investigation based on this evidence."

"That sounds like a step in the right direction," Eleanor said, leaning forward slightly in anticipation. "So what sort of evidence does the family think they have?"

"I believe I can explain best," spoke a soft, deep voice from just behind her. Eleanor froze instantly in her seat, a chill running down her spine as every hair on the back of her neck stood up in recognition. She knew that voice.

"Ah, Sergei," Kossakov greeted the man standing in the doorway behind her. "You have excellent timing, as usual. *Sadites pozhaluysta,* meet our American guest, Ms. Truman."

All she had to do was turn and her eyes would confirm what she already knew, but Eleanor sat still as stone. Her gaze fixed itself on Kossakov's cup of tea, tracing over the delicate pattern that'd been hand-painted along the rim. It sat on a matching saucer, the set exquisitely crafted from fine, white porcelain. Only half the dark liquid remained, but it settled in the cup with its surface smooth, calm and unperturbed the way Eleanor wished to remain. But panic spread adrenaline through her veins, and after skipping a beat, then two, her heart began to race beyond her control and she felt her face flushing with heat. Suddenly feeling choked for breath, she struggled to unfasten the top button at the collar of her blouse, unwilling to look at the man taking a seat in the chair beside her. Her breath came short as her heart beat a wild rhythm against her ribs; she felt like she might be sick.

Kossakov must have noticed because he called out urgently to Nadya, "*vodichku, bistrey!*"

A bottle of cool water was pressed into her hands by Kossakov's attentive assistant, and Eleanor took a long drink, grateful for the distraction. It gave her a few crucial moments to gather her composure before she raised her gaze to look at the man who had forever transformed her life.

"Are you alright?" he asked when she finally met his eyes. Three words had never sounded so loaded to her ear.

"I'm fine," she said, but her voice emerged as little more than a whisper. Intense and unrelenting, his gaze held hers across the minute distance between them, and Eleanor's heart ached sharply as she recognized the same blue hues she'd grown accustomed to seeing any time she looked at Ana.

Sergei hadn't changed. A new line or two around the edges, but his face and sandy-blonde hair remained the same. His broad jaw was softened by the stubble of a week's beard but that did nothing to hide the slight curve of his lips. He looked at her in a way that betrayed their familiarity, yet there wasn't a hint of surprise in the depth of his eyes.

CHAPTER V

Thief

When Mikhail Kossakov first called him to say that he'd brought on a young American psychologist to work up the profile of his sister's killer, Sergei hadn't thought much of it. But when the investigator said that her name was Eleanor Truman, the words brought his world to a sudden, screeching halt. It hit him like an earthquake, and left him shaken to the core. His first instinct was to have her fired, to make sure Kossakov sent her away on the very next flight out of the country. And yet, the thought that she was already there, located a mere stone's throw from his familial residence, was more than he could stand; it awoke a fire in his blood that'd lain dormant so long he'd nearly convinced himself it was dead.

So he'd come to the city, intent on seeing her at least once. As if that would ever be enough. He was kidding himself and he knew it, but he couldn't bring himself to stop. Not this time. Not when she was so close he could taste her.

What did he expect to see? Truth be told, he wasn't sure. A ring on her finger? Maybe. And what if there was?

There better not be.

He'd have been the first to admit that he had no right to expect anything from her–not after the way he'd up and left all those years ago. There was no doubt she must have looked for him; Eleanor was just that sort of girl. Sweet and kind and far too caring. Too easy for him to love, with her golden-brown hair in fine, curling strands and the doe-soft look in her gentle eyes. And he'd left all of that, without a word or warning, and made damn sure she would never find him. So the civilized part of him could accept the facts, but lord help him if there wasn't a savageness lurking beneath his civil veneer that threatened to tear apart anyone who dared to touch what was rightfully his.

She was more beautiful than he remembered. The first thing Sergei noticed when he took a seat in the chair beside Eleanor was that maturity suited her in a way that put her old photos to shame. Although, physically, she appeared practically the same, their time apart had most assuredly changed her. He couldn't identify exactly what it was, but the woman before him radiated a quiet strength and determination–and no little uncertainty about how to handle his unexpected appearance.

"I'm sorry," she apologized to Kossakov, tearing her gaze away from his, but Sergei saw a flash of torment she couldn't hide. "I think I need some fresh air. I'll just be a few minutes."

Refusing to look at him again, she rushed from the office, leaving Sergei and the investigator to exchange looks across the desk between them.

"Is everything okay?" Nadya asked from the doorway. "Should I follow her?"

"*Nyet, vse normalno,*" Sergei assured her. Addressing Kossakov, he continued, "*Izvinite menya,* Ms. Truman and I are formerly acquainted but seeing me must have come as a surprise. I'll go and check on her."

"*Ponyatno, khorosho,*" Kossakov said, following him with an appraising look as he stood and left the office.

He wasn't in a rush, but Eleanor hadn't made it very far. She was still waiting for the elevator at the end of the hall, and as he approached with measured, silent steps, the door slid open. In two quick steps he was behind her, seizing hold of her with an arm around her waist and his other hand over her mouth as he drug her into the empty elevator.

The door slid shut behind them and he leaned down to inhale the scent of her hair, a sweetly intoxicating blend of almond with macadamia, only to release her an instant later as she bit the palm of his hand. Hard.

"Nora," he growled, turning her around to stare at her in surprise. "Why?"

"Let go of me," she demanded at once, glaring up at him. "You're lucky I haven't kicked you in the balls or started screaming bloody murder. What the hell kind of way do you think that is to approach someone?"

There was genuine anger in her voice, a hard edge that was only softened by the look in her eyes as she stared up at him. It was a look of tenderness and anguish, forgiving and accusatory and full of confusion and pain all at the same time. He could see the girl who'd loved him in that moment, and it filled him with a sense of remorse he didn't know he could still feel.

"Where have you been?" she continued as tears clouded her eyes. Throwing her arms around his shoulders, she hugged him tightly and began to cry softly. "God, I thought you were dead."

"*Nyet, ya zhiv*," he replied, wrapping her in his arms. "*Prosti menya, dorogaya.* Shh, don't cry. Please don't cry over me."

That earned a bark of laughter from her, and Eleanor pulled her head away to swipe the sleeve of her shirt across her eyes. "Clearly your ego hasn't suffered. I'm not crying over you," well, technically she was, "I'm just... overwhelmed."

Pushing him away, she reached around him to hit the button for the ground floor and leaned back as the elevator began to descend.

"So," she stated, wiping her eyes again before leveling her watery stare on him. "It's good to know you're alive and well after all this time. I don't suppose you have an explanation for the last seven years?"

Sergei was silent for a minute, listening to each floor ding as they passed. What was he supposed to tell her?

"*Da niznayu ya*," he began, wanting to hedge around the subject.

"You'll have to repeat that in English," Eleanor said. "You left before I could pick up much more than *da* and *nyet.*"

"I said I don't know," he repeated with a sigh.

"Is that really the best you can come up with?" she asked, but didn't wait for an answer. "Would that be 'I don't know' as in you've suddenly recovered your memory after seven years of amnesia; or is it an 'I don't know' as in you're part of the thieves world and don't know want me to know?"

The elevator came to a stop just then and the doors slid open. Eleanor remained still for a moment, staring at him in expectation of a response, but when Sergei was silent she sighed heavily and left the elevator.

"Where are you going?" he asked, following her as she made a beeline for the main entrance. "Eleanor, how do you know about that?"

"I'm going outside because I need some fresh air to clear my head," she responded coolly. "And I know about it because I studied." Pushing open the main door, she stepped out onto the sunlit pavement, "I knew you were a liar when you said your tattoos didn't mean anything. So you're a thief?"

Sergei bristled, subconsciously clenching his jaw as the door swung shut behind them. Why couldn't she have been a normal girl and hated his guts after he left? It would have been easier than trying to explain the details of his murky past. Even if he wanted to tell her, he didn't have the slightest clue how to begin.

"That is what you'd call it in English," he finally said, facing her squarely as she leaned back against the building's concrete wall. "It's not what I am, though."

"Are you saying you aren't a thief in law?" she challenged. "Because I've heard they make men remove false tattoos."

His nostrils flared as he boxed her in against the wall, one hand on either side of her shoulders. Seven years apart hadn't made her any taller, so he easily towered over her by a full head and then some. Pressed between his broad-shouldered torso and the concrete wall behind her,

Eleanor had no choice but to tilt her head back in order to maintain eye contact with him.

"What?" she challenged, but her words came out as little more than a whisper.

"There is not a false mark on my body, Nora," he growled softly, leaning down to catch the scent of her hair again.

"I'm glad," she replied. "I would hate to see your body damaged."

Her words triggered a cascade of memories that made his chest ache sharply–the nights they'd spent tangled together, the feeling of her smooth, supple skin beneath his hands as she sighed his name. The touch of lips and teeth in the tenderest of places, distributing reverent kisses and love-bites in a patchwork of heated passion. Looking down at her, with her tear-streaked cheeks and strands of hair struggling loose from her pony-tail, he wanted to kiss her until her lips were swollen red and he'd stolen the breath from her lungs.

So he did.

CHAPTER VI

Flames

Eleanor felt like she'd been strapped to an emotional roller-coaster that was running at Mach speeds and refused to stop. A storm of conflicting feelings brewed within her, making her head swim. And then he kissed her. It was abrupt and intense, and it left her utterly breathless. Stunned but not unreceptive, she gripped the front of his jacket reflexively, pulling him closer as seven years of buried ardor roared to life.

His lips tasted of peppermint and beeswax, while something sweet and exotic lingered on his tongue. Somewhere in the back of her mind, the rational part of her protested that kissing him was the last thing she should be doing when he'd only reappeared five minutes ago, but it was swiftly drowned in the torrent of desire coursing through her veins. Every bit of repressed longing suddenly surged to the forefront and was poured into kissing him, an ardent exploration of his mouth that left her feeling positively electrified.

"Sergei," she breathed softly, two syllables warm against his lips. "We should stop."

"Then stop," he challenged, only to be silenced by her mouth closing over his. Wrapping her arms around his shoulders she kissed him a final time, as though her life depended on it, and then let go. Leaning back, she closed her eyes to focus on catching her breath.

"What are we doing here, Sergei?" she asked after a long moment, looking up at him.

"Reacquainting ourselves?" he offered. He was still watching her, deep blue eyes shining with intensity and his hands resting against the concrete on either side of her.

"That's not what I mean," she sighed, shaking her head. "I mean what are we doing here?" She gestured around them, indicating their surroundings in a general sense. "I'm supposed to be helping Mr. Kossakov profile a serial killer, and then you show up. Fine–it's my first time in Russia and it's only been, oh, seven years since you vanished into thin air, but okay... I just–fucking hell, I don't even know where to start. Where the hell have you been all this time?"

He exhaled through his nose, a long sigh that she recognized as meaning he had no idea what to say and would prefer not to answer at all.

"Fine, I'll make this easy for you," she said, shaking her head. "Have you been here, in Russia, for the last seven years?"

"*Da,*" he answered.

"And you left me because you're a thief in law?" she pressed, watching him shrewdly.

He shifted, clearly uncomfortable with either the substance of her questions or the location she chose to ask them. It was hard to tell which, or maybe it was both.

"*Da nyet,*" he answered obliquely.

"Did you?" Eleanor pressed. "I don't know what 'yes no' is supposed to mean."

"Yes, basically," he said.

There was no doubt her inquisition would have continued, but the main door of the building opened just then and Nadya stepped out. With her lips feeling tender from kissing him and Sergei still standing with his arms boxing her in, Eleanor felt her face light up scarlet in embarrassment as the other woman glanced them over.

"Mr. Ivanov, Ms. Truman," she greeted them politely, giving no indication that she'd even noticed their position as they straightened up, and Eleanor gave a silent prayer of thanks for her professionalism. "Mikhail Vadimovich suggested you might like to return to the hotel together to discuss the case, since Mr. Ivanov is familiar with all the details."

She had Eleanor's bag and the file from Kossakov's desk in her hand and held them out. "Shall I tell him you took his suggestion?"

Glancing from Nadya to Sergei and back again, Eleanor made a swift decision.

"Thank you, Nadya," she said, accepting her bag and the file. "Please tell Mr. Kossakov that I'm sorry our meeting ended so abruptly today. I'll email him as soon as I've had a chance to discuss the witness statement and any other pertinent details with Sergei." Her gaze settled back on him as she finished her statement.

There were about a thousand things going through her head, so she missed whatever it was that Sergei said to Nadya before she turned and left. Then they were alone again on the sidewalk and he turned to look at her. If she lived a thousand years, Eleanor was certain she would never forget how he looked just then. The years had changed him and yet he was the same, still the embodiment of her dreams with the warm summer sun falling on his mess of blonde hair and highlighting the varying shades of blue in his eyes. She'd lost herself in those endless depths before, it wasn't hard to imagine doing so again...

"So." He didn't break eye contact, but he didn't close the distance between them either. "What hotel did they put you in?"

"The Aurora Royale," she answered.

With the thread of their conversation having been interrupted by Nadya, the drive to her hotel was quiet. Sergei clearly knew his way through the city, making the return trip a swift one–or she was so caught up in her thoughts that she didn't notice the passage of time. It was mid-afternoon, so the hotel lobby was practically empty but the restaurant was open for lunch and they settled at a private table near the back.

"May I?" Sergei asked, indicating the menu.

"Hm?" Eleanor looked up. "Oh, yes, be my guest."

She was still recovering from the initial shock of meeting him, trying to reign in her thoughts. Every glance at him reminded her of Ana, but she bit her tongue. Kissing him back was one thing, revealing that he had a daughter was an entirely different matter and not one to rush. Searching for somewhere to let her gaze rest without meeting his eyes, she settled on the menu in his hands, with its golden lettering and lightly-worn corners. From the menu to his hands, her eye caught on the tattoo around his middle finger, a ring of ink that took the form of a regal crown. The contrast between the pitch black mark and his Nordic-white skin was stark, an effective reminder that he was not all the polished gentleman he appeared. A crown was the mark of a king, a leader in the criminal underworld. What had he done to earn such distinction?

"So, your sister," she finally said after he'd placed an order with their waiter. It was beginning to feel stilted and awkward, but she wasn't prepared to dredge up their entire past just yet. "You think she was deliberately targeted?"

"Without a doubt," he answered. "Olga was living with our mother while her husband traveled for work. In the weeks before she was murdered, our mother noticed someone following her on three occasions."

"Did she report it to the police?"

"Not at the time," he said.

"Why not?" she asked, looking at him in surprise.

"She thought perhaps they knew one another," Sergei answered.

"Why would she think that? I mean, why would someone follow her if they already knew one another?"

"Because she thought they might be having an affair," he stated bluntly. "And if she was having an affair, Olga would have been very discreet. She wasn't, though."

"You sound very sure," Eleanor observed.

"I am. I knew my sister well, and she was quite in love with her husband. They were never able to have their own children but they planned to adopt soon," he informed her. "Instead, she's dead and the one who did it is still out there, looking for more people to butcher."

"Are you going to kill him?" she asked. "I mean, if you find him. Isn't there a police investigation into this?"

"There is," Sergei agreed.

"And?"

"And nothing. If they catch him first, Russia has no death penalty but rest assured he'll get what he deserves," he said.

"Do you think they will?"

Their waiter returned with their drinks just then. Sergei remained silent until he'd left, then took a sip from his glass, looking at her the whole time.

"They might," he agreed. "I wouldn't hold my breath on the matter."

"Clearly," she sighed, leaning back. "I'm sure I wouldn't be here if you were willing to wait on the law."

"If you knew how the law here works, you wouldn't wait either," he said.

"Mmhm," she hummed, not impressed with his justification.

"You prefer to let more people die?" he queried her with a raised brow.

"No," she answered automatically.

"Then help me find him."

Over lunch they discussed the details of the case and his mother's witness statement, building a picture of their killer. Oksana said that the man who followed her daughter was well-dressed, with dark hair and a confident stride. She'd only spied him from a distance, and hadn't seen his face, but she was certain it was the same man on all three occasions. Average height, broad-shoulders, and he didn't seem overweight.

"So he could have been practically anyone," Eleanor sighed over her nearly-empty plate.

"That's why Mikhail called for an expert," Sergei pointed out.

"Oh don't worry, I'll figure this guy out," she assured him. "I just wish I had more to go on than the world's most generic description."

"I have no doubt in your skills," he said seriously. Finishing off his second drink, he set the glass aside with his empty plate. For a minute he was silent, just sitting there and regarding her from across the table as she shifted uneasily in her seat. Finally, he asked, "so what inspired you to study criminal psychology?"

"I think you know the answer to that question," she said.

"Pretend that I don't," he challenged. "Pretend we don't have any history beyond this case. What drew your interest to this field?"

"Fine," she sighed. "I always liked psychology, I think I had a natural knack for it, but what really got me into criminal psychology was a boyfriend I had."

"You don't sound very happy about him. What happened with him?"

She glared at him for a moment but then continued, "I was fresh out of high-school, pursuing a two-year arts degree at the community college while I decided what to really do with my life. He was a foreigner; a few years older than me, worldly, with these beautiful tattoos–" she paused to take a long drink, blinking fiercely as she looked at him. "We fell in love, but one day he vanished. When I looked for him, I learned what his tattoos meant, and from there one thing kind of led to another. Four years later I had my degree in criminal psychology."

"So you decided to stop looking?" he asked.

"I decided you were a liar or you had to be dead," she answered flatly, fighting to control the restless tapping of her foot. It was hard, sitting across from him and pretending that everything was normal. "Why else would you say so many things and then just disappear without a trace?"

"Aren't the greatest sacrifices usually made in the name of love?" he asked.

"Really?" she asked rhetorically. "You're going to use the 'I left because my life is too dangerous' excuse?"

"Is it such a bad excuse if its the truth?" he challenged.

"Except for the part where you knew what your life was like before you got involved with me," Eleanor whispered. "You knew what your life was like when you swore to cross the ends of the Earth for me. Not that I actually expected that, mind you–but you had no right to vanish like that. You owed me an explanation, at the very least."

"I may have," he conceded. "But you wouldn't have understood. It doesn't matter how much you've studied, you have no idea how dark the underside of this world is."

It was Eleanor's turn to regard him with her eyebrow askew.

"Are you serious?" she asked. "Who needs who in this investigation about his sister's murder, huh?"

"That's not what I'm referring to," he said.

"Well I'd consider it pretty fucking dark, thank you very much," she growled, picking up her fork to stab at the last remnants of noodles on her plate. "Are you trying to be a condescending prick? I was pretty naïve seven years ago, clearly!, but I've had time to mature and I'm not some delicate, wilting little flower that needs to be protected from the horrible, scary things in this world, thank you very much."

To her surprise, Sergei actually began to laugh lightly. It was a sound she'd almost entirely forgotten, and against her will she felt her heart swell with warmth at the sound. Lord help her, the man transformed when he smiled, from imposingly stern and professional to relaxed, even happy. But he seemed to be laughing at her, so she glared and resisted the urge to kick him beneath the table.

"What's so funny?" she demanded.

"Have you been waiting a long time to say that to me?" he asked. "It sounds like you've had plenty of practice." His laughter hadn't abated.

"Oh screw you," she sighed, sinking back in her seat to glare at him.

"Don't invite me unless you mean it," he warned her. Signaling their waiter over, he ordered a fresh drink and waited for the table to be cleared. When he turned his gaze back to her, Eleanor couldn't help the fierce blush that stained her cheeks. It was partly indignant anger, but mostly arousal.

"I wouldn't do that," she said, but she wasn't sure who she was trying to convince. "You're like fire. Burned once, twice shy."

"You don't seem so shy to me," he observed. Accepting his drink from their waiter, he set it on the table between them and looked at her meaningfully. "It won't be legal to drive if I enjoy the contents of this glass."

It was an invitation that made her spine tingle, and she knew she shouldn't take it. The right thing to do was to send him away, not ask him to stay.

"Maybe you should get a room for the night," she suggested.

"*Mozhet byt,*" he agreed. "But I'm afraid this hotel is booked solid."

"Then I guess you'll have to stay with me," she said.

CHAPTER VII

Possession

Seven years had done nothing to dampen his attraction to the woman before him. Something of her softness had gone, been replaced by the edges of a grown woman, but from the moment he looked at her, she became his red-lipped girl again. It didn't matter how hard she tried to hide it.

He downed his drink without taking his gaze from her, fueled by the desire in her shining eyes. Leaving money on the table, he rose and extended his hand to her. "Lead the way."

The elevator was waiting idly on the ground floor when they reached it, as if it anticipated their arrival. Eleanor found the button for her floor and pressed it; she trembled slightly, standing beside him as the door closed and the lift rose.

"Relax," he said softly, seeking to reassure her. Wrapping an arm around her shoulders, he pulled her close to his side and began rubbing her upper arm gently. "I promise not to ravish you." His fingertips ran down her back, feeling the smooth line of her spine through the fabric of her shirt.

"It's not that," she whispered, shaking her head.

"What, then?" he asked, then groaned as the obvious occurred to him. "Don't tell me you have a boyfriend after the way you kissed me."

Her face lit up red. "The way I kissed you?"

The elevator dinged open on their floor, so he waited until they made it to her room. Letting the door swing shut behind them, he turned immediately to press her back against it.

"*Da,*" he whispered, nuzzling the hair above her ear as he sought her hands with his and gripped them gently. "The way you kissed me."

Leaning down, he caught her mouth in another kiss, intent on quenching his thirst for her this time. Drawing her lower lip between his teeth, he bit it tenderly, then reached out with the tip of his tongue to tease past her teeth and caress the roof of her mouth. She responded eagerly to him, deepening their kiss with a quiet moan.

"The way you're kissing me now," he growled softly against her lips. Pulling away, he stared down at her seriously. "I didn't hear any vociferous protestations of innocence. Do you have a boyfriend?"

"No," she answered instantly this time, but she looked away from him and he could see a flash of regret pass through her eyes.

"Then what?" he pressed.

"Then nothing," she said, struggling to loose her hands from his grip in order to reach up to his shoulders. "It's just hard to believe you're here after so long. I never thought I'd see you again. Why, do you have a girlfriend?"

"*Nyet,*" he answered, shaking his head.

"A wife, perhaps?" she asked, reaching for his left hand to check for a ring.

"We wear it on the right," he informed her, raising his bare hand for her to see. "Still no."

"Mm, that's good." Leaning up, she ran her hands through his hair and kissed him again. It was slow, sensual and soul-stealing, and it made him ache in longing for the years they'd lost. Something else ached, too, the length of his shaft swollen hard and confined within his pants. And the fact that he could feel her breasts pressed soft against his chest through their clothes didn't help.

Pulling away from him, Eleanor stepped out of her low heels and slipped past to precede him into the room. She'd left the heavy, outer blinds open so the sun could shine through the sheer privacy curtains, and late afternoon light filled the suite. It illuminated her hair, bringing out tones of golden and bronze on dark mahogany. The first time he asked if it was natural, she'd sworn she never colored or dyed it, and he was inclined to believe her.

Toeing off his shoes, he followed her toward the bed, tossing his suit jacket across the small couch near the door. Eleanor set her bag in the doorway, backing up with her eyes on him the whole time. Fueled by a combination of passion and the vodka making its way through his blood, he advanced on her until the back of her legs hit the edge of the bed. With a gentle nudge, he knocked her down on her back and sank to his knees before her. Resting a warm hand over each of her knees, he stroked her gently through the thin fabric of her skirt. Trailing his hands lower, he reached for the skirt's hem and lifted it slowly, just far enough to reveal her knees. Bending his head, he pressed a kiss to each of her kneecaps, nuzzling her delicate skin through the sensible nude stockings she wore.

It was wrong to get involved with her again when it couldn't last. He knew it, but he couldn't bring himself to stop. Leaving her the first time was the hardest thing he'd ever done in his life. How would he ever bring himself to do it again?

"I don't know how I let go of you before," he groaned, leaning his forehead against her knees. The scent of her skin permeated his nostrils, an erotic blend of something floral with light, sweet musk that was purely her. It aroused buried memories of their stolen time together and made his balls tighten in excitement at the same time. Finger-walking his way slowly up her thighs, he reached to the top of her stockings and caught the material in order to drag it down. An inch at a time, he exposed her creamy skin, reveling in the soft sighs that escaped her lips. Grazing his nails over her sensitive flesh as he went, he continued until he'd rolled her stockings clear down to her toes before tossing them aside.

Lifting each of her legs by the ankle, he kissed the tops of her feet, then her ankles and shins. Massaging their way over her calves, his hands trailed back up and he had an irresistible urge to tickle the back of her knees. She shrieked in surprise and jerked automatically at the touch, sitting up as he desisted.

"Don't do that!" she admonished him. "You know I can't stand to be tickled."

"Just checking," he said. Releasing one of her knees, he reached up to cup the side of her face and drew her close for another kiss. His other hand remained, the tips of his fingers stroking slow circles over her kneecap.

As they kissed, Eleanor's hands moved from her lap to the front of his shirt. Stumbling fingers worked each button loose until the garment could be eagerly pulled open. Her hands were soft when she touched his skin, spreading a feeling like electric fire over his whole body. With a groan, he broke away from her lips, reaching simultaneously to loose her ponytail, releasing her hair to cascade over her shoulders and back in fragrant waves.

"When did you cut it?" he asked, running his fingers loosely through the silken mass. It used to hang to her hips like an auburn curtain but now stopped just below her shoulder blades.

"Years ago," she answered. "I needed a change after you left, something to help me feel–I don't know. Different, I suppose. It was pretty extreme at first, I started with a total pixie cut about that long." She held her fingers roughly two inches apart to demonstrate.

"What were you thinking?" he asked. "Did you like it?"

"Oh no, it was awful," she answered with a pained laugh. "I thought it would help me feel stronger, like a real independent power woman, but it didn't work. I liked it for about a day, and then spent a month crying because I couldn't undo what I'd done. My mother had to cover the mirrors for a while just to keep me from weeping at the sight of it."

"*Dorogaya,*" he sighed. Resting his forehead against hers, he caressed her cheek gently with the pad of his thumb. He could see the misting of tears that clouded her eyes at the memory. "I believe the phrase is cutting your nose to spite the face?"

His comment earned a wry smile from her.

"To say the least," she agreed. "The worst part wasn't even the original cut, but that awful stage when I started growing it back, somewhere between too-long-to-style and not-long-enough for braids or pony-tails. And the bangs! Lord save me from bangs, I cannot stand how they get loose and mess about in my face. Oh, it was hell."

"It sounds positively tragic," he agreed. He tried to picture her with short hair, but it was impossible to conjure a mental image. "At least it grew back. You could have done something truly drastic, like get a tattoo."

His humor wasn't lost on her.

"I thought about it," she said, her gaze sliding down to the tattoo on his hand and then up to the hint of dark ink that curled over his shoulder. She wet her lips, a pink flash of her tongue that aroused a heady mix of sensations below his belt.

"What stopped you?"

Her eyes jumped back to his, then slid away for a moment before returning. "I guess I thought I'd never be able to forget you if I did."

"Ah, I see," he said, letting his hands fall to her shoulders. She'd worn a sleeveless blouse that left her shoulders bare, cool to the touch against his palms as he trailed his hands down to her elbows and back. "And did you?"

"What?" she asked distractedly.

"Forget me," he answered.

His words were greeted by a soft snort and the shaking of her head.

"Of course not." She leaned forward, close enough to kiss him, but stopped short just as their lips brushed and their breaths mingled. "You proved to be regrettably unforgettable."

"Regrettably?" he asked, surprised by her choice of words.

"Mmhm," she confirmed quite seriously. "I can count the number of lousy dates I've been on in the last seven years on one hand and I blame you. You ruined me for other men."

"I see," his mouth grazed against hers as he spoke. "That's quite an accusation." Not that he was complaining. After the way he'd left, he knew he had no rightful claim over her, but the thought of anyone else touching her was enough to ignite a jealous flame in him. If she wanted to claim she'd never been able to move on from him, then all the better.

"It isn't an accusation," she corrected him. "Just a statement of truth."

"Then I shall have to make up for it," he said and kissed her again.

"Mm, I'm not sure you can," she sighed against his lips.

"That won't stop me from trying," he responded.

CHAPTER VIII

Surrender

In the back of her mind, a small voice of reason cautioned Eleanor to slow down. It was wrong to become lovers again before she told him about Ana. But she had no intention of telling him. Not yet. A strong protective instinct held her back, fearful of what the consequences might be if she revealed the truth. At the end of the day, Sergei was still a criminal. How far would he go if he knew, and how could she stop him?

The thought of how powerless she would be against him should have been sobering but it only served to arouse her more. It made her hot at the core, slick with anticipation for him. *God, what a deviant I've become.*

Whatever his status was in the criminal world, the callouses on his palms belied the fact he worked with his hands as they grazed over the sensitive skin of her thighs, hitching her skirt higher. A few inches more and his fingertips found the elastic hem of her panties, sliding under to tug the fabric out of his way. The breath rushed from her lungs in a half-sigh, half-moan of desire and, eager to feel the heat of his skin against her own, she tugged his shirt off entirely.

"*Moya krasavitsa,*" he smiled as he spoke, a corner-mouthed grin that flashed the perfect row of his upper teeth. It was Ana's smile. Her chest tightened and for a split second she felt her voice rise in her throat before she swallowed the sound.

"Speak English," she asked him instead.

"*Nyet, ne budu,*" he growled, letting the weight of his upper body press her down gently as he leaned over her. His gaze was intense and tender at the same time. "*Moya dusha pusta bez tebya.*"

"And now in English?" she prompted.

"*Nyet,*" his breath warmed her ear as he denied her. "*Poslushay menya, milaya*–why are you here, tempting me?"

"Isn't that what I should be asking you?" she challenged, reaching for his belt.

"Only if it's the truth," he answered. Stilling her hands, he unbuckled his belt for her.

"More than anything," she affirmed, flicking loose the button at his waist. Slowly, deliberately, she unzipped the front of his pants.

An act that'd seemed so simple and insignificant to her before suddenly felt unspeakably intimate, even erotic. She could feel the rigid length of his erection straining through the fabric between them, foreign and yet familiar. Sliding her hand into his pants, she let the back of her knuckles and hand stroke against his cock through the silken fabric of his boxers, a fleeting touch before she slid his pants down for him to kick off.

"Still a cocktease," he observed, following her as she slid further up the bed. When her head hit the pillows, she stopped and he grasped her hand, drawing it back down to rest warmly against his confined shaft.

"Touch me," he urged her. "I haven't forgotten how much you love my cock."

His confidence that this fact remained unchanged was strangely arousing, and in any case she wasn't going to deny the truth.

"Mm, I'm sure," she agreed, drawing him into a kiss. It wasn't hard to free him from the prison of silk so she could wrap her fingers around the smooth, hard length of his flesh. "Do you remember how I used to suck you dry?" She knew he did, the fact his cock throbbed hard in response was only confirmation. "And then we'd rest for a while before you'd find my mouth wrapped around you again, sucking you hard so you could fuck me some more."

"*Blyat,*" he swore softly, covering her hand with his and squeezing. "Of course I haven't forgotten."

She knew he was containing the urge to ejaculate all over her hand, could feel the rhythmic throbbing in his veins that belied just how aroused he was. It filled her with a rush of endorphins and reciprocal arousal. If she'd been slick between the thighs before, she was soaking now. Empowered, she nudged his hand away and began to stroke slowly up and down the length of his cock.

"I bet you've thought of me when you touch yourself," she whispered. The words felt devious and dirty just leaving her mouth, heightening her lust.

"Of course," he readily agreed. It was his turn to put her on edge as his hand returned to the apex of her thighs, the tips of his fingers dancing over her swollen pubic mound. He gripped her through the fabric of her skirt first, eliciting a moan as her hips jerked upward. "*Da,* you want it too.

"How many nights have you slid your fingers into your pussy and wished it was me stretching you instead?" Stroking into her hand to emphasize his words, he flipped her skirt out of the way and slid his hand between her bare legs. "How many times did you wake on the edge of orgasm, haunted by memories of me?"

"Oh god Sergei," she panted, unable to catch her breath or still the racing of her heartbeat. "You play dirty."

"I play with fire," he corrected, then kissed her silent as he slid the tip of his finger past her labia to tease at her hot entrance. Breaking from her mouth, he continued, "you're so wet, pussy all soft and slick, ready for me. Deny me, or I'm going to fuck you until we both collapse."

"When will you ever learn?" she moaned, pressing down against his hand. The tip of his finger had penetrated her, but just barely. He held back, even as his cock twitched madly against her palm.

"I want to hear you say it," he said.

"I could never deny you," she panted, "and you know it."

"*Konechno,*" he agreed, and kissed her, moving his hand and shifting their bodies to align himself with her slick, sensitive entrance. "I still like to hear you say it."

He slid forward, penetrating her slowly, sinking deeper as she stretched to accommodate him. It'd been years since she used much more than her own hands to find relief; what a difference it made to have him with her again, to feel the press of his skin against hers as he moved over her, within her, the blood surging through his veins for her.

It was dark when he awoke. Sergei rolled onto his back, stretching his arm out to find his lover in the darkness. Finding only empty sheets, he sat up and tossed the bedding aside.

His eyes were well-adjusted to the darkness, quickly picking out the door that divided her suite. It was shut, but light leaked around the doorframe and he could hear Eleanor speaking softly in the other room. In half a stride he could rest his hand on the knob but he paused, able to pick out the words of her conversation.

"... more than a week," she was saying. "As soon as I finish this job, I'll be on my way back." She paused but he didn't hear anyone respond; she had to be on the phone. The prospect that she was speaking to another man incensed him. He inhaled slowly through his nose, hand clenching tightly around the doorknob as he resisted the urge to tear it off the wall and confront her.

"Yes—on the calendar," Eleanor continued. It was hard to pick out what she was saying but the very fact she was trying to conceal something from him was enough to make him see red. Twisting slowly, he eased the door open a crack.

"—good. It's late here, I have to go now," soft as she spoke, her voice was crystal clear with the door open. "I love you, good night."

Giving the door a tug so that it swung freely open, he leaned in the doorway to watch as she froze before him. Her already fair skin became worryingly pale, and after a moment of inaction she opened her mouth to say something only to close it again in silence.

"Mm *da, interesno,*" he observed, remaining where he was as he watched her. Interesting indeed. "*Skazhi pozhaluysta, komu ty zvonila?*"

"I don't understand," she said, shaking her head though the look in her eyes told him otherwise.

"Who did you call?" he repeated, indicating the phone still clutched in her hand.

Her eyes flicked away from him, a moment of hesitation that screamed deception. He'd been around thieves and liars long enough to pick up on even the slightest indication of dishonesty. It was a skill that'd kept him alive more times than he could count, and one that'd helped him avoid sinking into depressive paranoia like so many of the men he'd known.

"I was just talking to my mom," she answered. Like her eyes, her voice gave her away, sounding tight and uncertain as she shifted her weight back to her heels.

"Uh-huh," he made no effort to contain his disbelief. "And you needed to do this so quietly that I would not hear?"

"Well no." She swallowed. "You were sleeping, I didn't want to wake you."

"*Ladno,*" he sighed. "Give me your phone."

He extended his hand. Eleanor hesitated, leaning back as though she would withdraw further from him, and he resisted the urge to seize it directly from her.

"Why? Don't you trust me?" she asked.

"*Nu da,* I trust you," he informed her, "but you're lying. Now hand me the phone."

CHAPTER IX

Brothers

It only took Sergei a moment to swipe through her call log once Eleanor handed her phone to him. Or partially threw, as the case may be. She hated being called a liar, even if it was technically true. But she wasn't about to confess that she'd been on the phone with their six-year-old daughter.

"Well?" she demanded, staring at him expectantly. The aggression was a cover for how nervous she felt every moment he held onto her phone. What if he decided to test her mother's number by dialing it? Even if Ana didn't race to answer the phone, Eleanor didn't want to deal with the potential of her mother picking up either.

Sergei's gaze lingered on the screen a moment longer as he calculated something, then flicked back to her.

"I'm sorry," he said, handing her phone back. "I spoke too soon."

"Uh-huh." She stared at him, trying to maintain a cool appearance. It was hard to do, especially when she realized he hadn't bothered to put on a stitch of clothing. "When did you become so suspicious?"

"It comes with the territory," he answered, leaning against the doorframe. "Why did you look so nervous when I opened the door?"

"You just startled me, that's all," she said.

"Is it?"

"Yes," she looked down, trying to avoid staring at his groin, and her gaze fell to the eight-pointed stars tattooed on each of his knees. *I kneel to no one.* Indeed.

"*Izvini,*" he apologized. Following her gaze, he asked deviously, "see something you like?"

Eleanor's eyes swept back up to meet his. Setting her phone aside, she closed the distance between them in two small steps to place her hands on his chest. Trailing her fingertips over his skin, she leaned up against him and laid a tender kiss at the corner of his smirking mouth.

"*Nyet,*" she said, breathing soft against his lips. Reaching lower, she took hold of him intimately, feeling him swell in her hand. "I see someone I love."

He wrapped an arm around her, drawing her tighter against his bare torso. "Careful who you profess to love," he warned.

"I am," she assured him. Removing her hand, she kissed him properly, then pulled away to step past him. "But I think you should go now."

"Oh really?" He sounded surprised as he shifted, turning to watch as she clicked the light on.

"Yes," she affirmed. "I've still got a job to do, so I need to sleep and I can tell that's not going to happen with you here." Her eyes flicked back over him as she collected his clothes from the floor. "As pleasurable as that might be, it won't do anything to stop your serial killer from striking again. So I need to work, which means you have to go."

"Let me shower first," he said.

"Not a chance," Eleanor laughed, tossing his shirt at his face. His pants followed a moment later. "You can shower at home. Come on, get dressed."

"Oy," he protested but complied with her order, tugging his shirt over his head with a theatrical rolling of his eyes. "You drive a cold bargain."

"I'm sure," she said, nodding. "Here are your socks."

"Nora," he breathed, catching her in his arms and pulling her close. "Are you upset at me?"

"No," she answered honestly, giving him a soft kiss. "But I do need to work. So give me your number and go, I'll call you tomorrow if I have any questions."

"As you wish," he agreed. "And when may I return to have lunch with you?"

"Not tomorrow," she said. "I don't know. The day after maybe. I've got to think about this case."

"*Ladno,* call me when you're ready." He kissed her again, then finished dressing and donned his shoes by the door.

Eleanor watched him go, leaning in the same spot he'd stood minutes before. Her heart was still racing, lips tender from kissing, when he cast her a final look and shut the door. The lock clicked into place automatically and she listened for a moment as he walked away. Going to the window, she looked down into the street, waiting for him. When he stepped onto the sidewalk a few minutes later, he turned and seemed to look directly up at her. Then he turned, greeted the valet who pulled around with his car, took the wheel, and drove away.

When he arrived home, Sergei was greeted at the door by one of his oldest friends and adopted brother, Pavel Konstantinovich. Known to friends and family as Pasha, he was also the head of Sergei's private security, and for good reason. The man was intimidatingly large, with broad shoulders and forearms thicker than a young birch tree; but his sheer, imposing size wasn't what Sergei valued most about his friend. Pasha possessed a shrewd, calculating mind, and was hawkishly attentive to his surroundings. He was also loyal, to the laws of their thieves' code and to the family who delivered him from a life of certain ruin.

"You're back late," Pasha observed when Sergei entered, shrugging out of his lightweight jacket to hang it near the door. Pasha was sitting in the small room adjacent to the entry with a teapot and half-empty cup on the table next to an empty plate and a closed book. It was his preferred spot to wait if a member of the household wasn't accounted for, and keeping him company beneath the table was Brutus, a huge black mutt they'd found on the streets as a puppy and raised to be a guard at the house.

Sergei kicked off his shoes, remaining silent until he finished changing into his house slippers. He leaned against the doorway, greeting Brutus with a scratch on the head when the dog rose to welcome him home.

"Business in the city," he finally said.

"How is the investigator?" Pasha asked, referring to Kossakov.

"He brought a specialist," Sergei answered. "We'll have the bastard soon."

"Good, progress," he said. "Masha left food for you in the oven."

"Join me for a drink," Sergei suggested, motioning toward the kitchen.

"Are we celebrating something?" he asked, rising from his seat. Brutus followed the men, trailing a few steps behind them as they crossed through the foyer and into the kitchen.

"Yes and no," Sergei said, retrieving a pair of shot glasses and a bottle of vodka from a cupboard. He put the items on the table and set about retrieving the food Pasha's wife had left. A bowl of sausage-filled dumplings and a pan of meat pies that were still slightly warm in the center had been left in the oven, covered with cloth to keep the food from drying out. Fresh dill pickles, a dish of black caviar, and a jar of pickled eggs completed the table setting and the men took their seats. Brutus, loyal companion that he was, assumed his position beneath the table, curling his impressive bulk into an astoundingly compact ball of warmth between their feet.

"Good boy," Pasha praised the dog, handing him a meat pie from the tray.

"You spoil him," Sergei admonished him lightly, uncapping the vodka bottle.

"Impossible," his friend pronounced. "He won't even take shish kebab from a stranger, and he's waited for his master to return for dinner. You couldn't buy a better beast."

"The beast has an entire fridge full of meat in the basement. Let him cook his own pies," Sergei asserted humorously. Having filled their shot glasses, he raised his with a much more serious look in his eyes. "To Kossakov's specialist. I will put the son of a bitch into so many pieces not a single soul will be able to identify him."

Pasha toasted him and downed the shot, then commented, "I gather the business went well today? You haven't been so optimistic in a while."

"Indeed," Sergei agreed, filling their glasses again. Taking one of the meat pies, he spread a spoonful of caviar across the top and took a bite, then reached for the pickled eggs. "We need salt and pepper."

Pasha twisted, reaching behind him to the nearby counter. The salt and pepper were well within reach of his long arms and he passed them to Sergei.

"Thank you." He set the lid aside and took a pinch of salt, sprinkling it liberally over an egg. "Is Dima back yet?"

"No, he needs two more days. Turns out the well is clogged so he's going to clean it out," Pasha said. "Unless you intend to drink from the pond, of course."

As soon as he'd learned that Eleanor was in the country, Sergei had tasked the third man in their close-knit group, Dimitri Lomonosov, with going to his family's countryside cottage in order to clean it up. It was good timing, too. While Pasha was happily married to a woman who understood the demands of his life, Dima maintained a strained relationship with the temperamental daughter of a small-town prosecutor. They'd been on-again, off-again for the better part of five years and had gotten into another fight recently. Something about the potential (or lack thereof) for marriage or children, probably both. Sergei wasn't up-to-date on the details of their latest spat but it was all the excuse he needed to send Dima to the village for a few days.

"Good," he paused to drink another shot and then continued, "I have another task for him when he's finished. Anything new on Sverlov?"

"*Phoo*," Pasha mock spat and downed another shot. "No news. The bastard's gone quiet, hiding out. No one's seen him since the night he left."

"There's no need to insult him," Sergei corrected him mildly, pouring out another set of shots. "He's trying to look after his own interests, same as anyone would."

"Bullshit," Pasha disagreed. "What, are we hooligans? No. So why is he on the run? We're willing to make a reasonable deal."

"Drink," Sergei suggested, clinking glasses with him again. "Don't break your head on him for now. Just keep your ears open, he'll make a mistake."

Yuriy Sverlov. Six months ago, if he'd been asked to pick who was most likely to betray the family, Sergei would never have put Yuriy first. As children, they'd called him *dyadya*–uncle. Well, Sergei and Dima had called him that anyway. Pasha had never fully warmed up to their father's closest friend and partner in the criminal world. *Dyadya* Yura was a trusted member of their criminal family though, close enough that everyone had been certain Sergei would someday marry one of his daughters to complete the bond. With three daughters to choose from, each of them intelligent and beautiful, it hadn't seemed like such a far-off idea.

For years, the favorite choice for a match had been Yuriy's youngest daughter, Lila. Despite the fact that she was nearly a full decade his junior, Lila had grown up with an unrivaled adoration for Sergei. By the time she reached adolescence, her childhood adoration had taken on a distinctly romantic flavor and she practically worshipped the ground he walked on. He'd been eternally grateful when the amorous girl was sent to a finishing school at fourteen, not to return until she was a legal woman.

But all good things had to end. When she reached eighteen, Lila returned to Moscow with a mind to marry. Empowered by Yuriy's approval of the match and his own father's fondness for her, headstrong Lila had brought the matter to Sergei fully expecting that he would agree. And perhaps he should have.

But he didn't, and it was causing him more problems than he'd foreseen.

Part of it was the fact that, try as he might to forget the child he'd watched grow up, Sergei had never been able to shake off the feeling that Lila was like a little sister to him. All three of Yuriy's daughters were like that to him, and they'd been extremely close to Olga, who acted as an older sister to everyone in the family. No one in their right mind would marry their sister, and that's what he'd insisted upon when he refused the match.

It was the truth, but not entirely. By the time Lila returned, he'd already been to the United States for a year. Like a dutiful son, he'd gone there to study and look for opportunities the family might use to expand their business interests internationally. He'd never expected to lose part of his soul in the process.

CHAPTER X

Threads

The sun had risen high in the sky by the time Sergei awoke the next day. He would have continued sleeping, but Masha cracked his door open and let Brutus into the room to rouse the master from his bed. She leaned in the doorway as he attempted to hide from the dog's slobbery, enthusiastic affection.

"Oy, Mash—why?" he groused, sitting up and pulling Brutus into a friendly headlock.

"You're lucky I let you sleep at all," she informed him with a stern look. "I don't appreciate it when my husband comes to bed reeking like a drunk."

"Yes, you can blame me for that," Sergei acknowledged, scratching Brutus' head and rubbing behind his ears. "Forgive me, Maria Alexandrovna, but you know it's not good to drink alone."

"Ha," she scoffed. "It's not good to drink at all."

"Maybe," he acquiesced.

"So what were you celebrating?" she asked.

"Who said I was celebrating?" he replied.

"Oy," Masha sighed, rolling her eyes. "You were celebrating, or someone died." She paused as her own words sparked a thought. "Or maybe you were celebrating because someone died?"

"No one died," Sergei said. Scrubbing his hands over his face, he rubbed his eyes clear and then ran a hand through his hair, straightening the haphazard mess if only slightly. "Inspector Kossakov brought a specialist to help us resolve my sister's case."

"I see," Masha said, nodding in understanding though her eyes remained full of disapproval. "Next time wait to celebrate, it's too early for toasts."

Sergei wasn't going to argue with her, especially given the fact that he agreed. He wouldn't drink to his sister until she was avenged, but he also wasn't going to confess that he'd found Eleanor. No one in his family knew about the American girl who stole his heart, he'd never told them and that wasn't about to change.

"Right you are, Masha," he said. "Was there anything else you wanted to reprimand me for this morning?"

"Is there something else I should be reprimanding you for?" she asked, regarding him with suspicious scrutiny. For a woman who had only been married to Pasha for three years, Masha had managed to settle herself into their household of brothers with astonishing alacrity. It was probably because they'd long been accustomed to living with a woman in the house, so in the years after they began living alone it always felt that there was something missing. That something turned out to be someone, and Masha entered the home as a wife and sister. A sister who now had no compunction about scolding her brothers when they misbehaved.

"No, nothing," Sergei assured her.

"You know I'll find out if there is," she warned him.

"Of course," he agreed. "That's why I tell you, from an honest heart, there is nothing. So what's for breakfast?"

"Lunch," she corrected. "And nothing for you until you bathe."

Sergei lifted an arm, sniffing and then gagging theatrically. "It was my goal that enemies smell me a mile in the wind, but since you insist."

"I do," Masha said with a laugh. "Alright, I left clean clothes for you in the bathroom. Come on Brutus, your master needs to take a bath."

Lunch consisted of potatoes, leftover meat pies from the night before, and pickled cabbage with salt. Pasha was already seated at the table when Sergei emerged, his hair still damp from the shower. A loaf of bread, platter of sliced fruits for dessert, and carafe of hot tea waiting to be poured were the final touches to a well-prepared table.

"Woken with a scolding, yet rewarded like a king," Sergei remarked to Pasha, settling into his chair at the head of the table. "Your wife is a strange creature."

"His wife hears you," Masha commented, emerging from the kitchen with their plates and glasses. She set them on the table before the men, reaching into her pocket for their silverware.

"With ears like a bat," Sergei added.

"And trust me," she continued, "if I thought starvation would reform the lot of you, I'd have no qualms about it. Since that won't work, eat, be healthy. I'm a resourceful woman, I'll find something that works on you."

"Oh-ho, you'd better watch out," Pasha chuckled, helping himself to the first of several pies. "She sounds serious."

Sergei shook his head, pouring out their tea. "I believe she was addressing us both, in which case I feel it must be said that you married her."

Masha took her seat, laughing as Pasha made a face. It felt good to relax with his family, but Sergei's thoughts were divided and he settled into silent contemplation as they ate. Long accustomed to such behavior, Pasha and Masha continued a conversation between themselves, leaving Sergei to think.

Dima wouldn't be back from the dacha until the end of the weekend, at the earliest. Meanwhile, there hadn't been any sign of Yuriy in nearly two weeks. His sister's case was unresolved. And all the time, thoughts of Eleanor kept clouding his mind. The taste of her, the scent of her, the trembling undulations of her body and rush of her breath as she climaxed with him. It took enormous willpower for him not to return to her. He'd barely been able to leave the night before but the prospect of Pasha coming out or sending someone to find him had brought him home.

It didn't help matters that his desire for Eleanor was mixed with suspicion. Her call log had confirmed that she'd been on the phone with her mother, and at a glance he hadn't seen any male names in her recent calls. That should have satisfied him but it didn't. Her reaction to seeing him had been too strong, it reeked of fear. It couldn't be fear of him, not the way she reacted to his tattoos and other reminders of his shaded past. If she was afraid of him, she wouldn't look at him the way she did, wouldn't react to him like she'd finally returned to the place she belonged. Beside him. Beneath him. Yet she was hiding something. He stifled a growl of frustration, tearing off a chunk of bread from the loaf.

"Call Anton when we finish," he instructed Pasha. "And arrange a bouquet of flowers."

"Oh?" Pasha looked to him with a raised brow. "For who?"

Masha was listening too, suddenly quite interested.

"Lila," he growled. "So make sure there are lilacs in the bouquet. And some of that godforsaken chocolate she loves, a small box."

"Are you trying to bribe her?" Masha asked. She looked, and sounded, skeptical.

"I need her to talk to me." Sergei nodded. "Do you have any suggestions?"

"Perhaps," she said. "What's your goal?"

"She knows where her father is hiding," he answered.

"Maybe," Masha agreed. "But maybe not. Do you really think she'll tell you for a bouquet of flowers and a box of chocolate?"

"Only if she's had a partial-lobotomy recently," he stated. "I've known her since she was born, she's stubborn but she'll talk to me. The flowers and chocolate are just a courtesy."

"Have you talked to her since your father died?" she challenged. "Because before that, I seem to recall a prolonged, icy silence that began after you refused to marry the poor girl."

Pressing his lips into a thin line, Sergei didn't say anything. It was true that Lila had not reacted well to the news. She'd withdrawn from any mutual obligations that might have brought them into contact, and steadfastly ignored him if they happened to cross paths. And he hadn't made any serious effort to break the silence while his father was still alive, concerned that any renewal of his friendship with Lila would spark new hopes of their eventual marriage. It'd been nearly a year since his father died though and despite the fact that they'd both spoken at the funeral, Sergei still hadn't made direct contact with her.

"She will talk," he stated again. Or he would make her.

"Give her a piece of jewelry," Masha advised. "Something personal and tasteful, you have a good eye for these things. She's young, beautiful, give her a gemstone necklace with matching earrings."

"Woah, Masha," Pasha interrupted. "I don't think he's changed his mind about marrying her. Seryozha?"

"No," Sergei agreed. "But it's not so far off. Lila has always been like a sister to us, and a brother may give his sister jewelry."

"Uh-huh." Pasha sounded distinctly unconvinced. "Tell that to her."

"I will," Sergei said. "You just arrange the flowers and chocolate. And call Anton."

"Understood," Pasha said. "Chocolate, lilacs, a shovel."

Sergei raised an eyebrow at him.

"To help you dig your grave," Pasha elaborated. "You'll need it, brother."

"And call Anton," Sergei repeated.

"I'll call Anton," Pasha grumbled. "When do you want him?"

"As soon as he can pull himself together properly," Sergei instructed. "And for the love of god tell him to be discreet."

Anton Pechenkin liked to drive too fast and drink too much, among his lesser sins. Those particular two were not a good combination though, and there was little in life Sergei disliked so much as having to deal with the countless, petty infractions his father's last protégé perpetrated in the course of his daily life. For some insane reason, Lila had always gotten along with Anton though, and the boy–for he could hardly be called a man with the entirely immature ways he behaved– proved useful from time to time. Now would be one of those times, and since he owed his life in service to the family, Anton would obey.

In the meantime, he had a jewelry purchase to make. Masha's suggestion for Lila was one that he readily accepted, but it also provided an excellent excuse to shop for Eleanor. Seven years ago, the idea of gifting her jewelry hadn't even occurred to him. Now it appealed to him as a modern, accepted way to mark her that aroused his primal side. The right piece would send a perfect, unmistakable message. She belongs to someone else, stay away.

And she did. Whether she realized it or not. He would burn for a thousand years, let his soul be consumed by fire, but he would never renounce his claim on her. Every time he closed his eyes, he saw her or some part of her. Cheekbones, lips, the silhouette of her hips. For seven years he had subsisted on memories and little more. Having her back, lingering so close, left him positively intoxicated.

"I'll be back in a few hours," he informed Pasha, rising from the table when he'd finished eating.

"If Anton arrives while you're gone?"

"He can wait for me," Sergei said. "And don't let him idle, give him something useful to do."

"Like what?" Pasha asked.

Sergei shrugged. "Masha can decide. The house is full of chores. Just keep him here. And get the other things."

"Yes, most honorable liege," Pasha replied sarcastically, bowing deeply from his seat. "We live to serve. And where, pray tell, are you going?"

"To pick out something for Lila," he answered.

"You're gonna give her the wrong idea!" Pasha called after him as he left.

His brother's advice came from the heart, but he knew Lila better than anyone. As a kid she'd just been adorable and sweet, not horny and crazy. That phase had started later, in her teenage years when hormones started driving her wild. If he could just reach her, get through to the part of her that loved and trusted him as a brother instead of trying to make him the focal point of her romantic fantasies, then he would be able to enlist her help. And as loathe as he was to deal with her, he needed Lila's help if he wanted to negotiate with Yuriy. The whole drama had begun within the family, it had to end within the family.

CHAPTER XI

Entangled

It was late afternoon when Sergei returned. The family's Moscow residence was located just north of the city, an old manor that'd been restored by his father during the chaos of the 90s. Sergei rolled down the gravel drive to find a familiar black sports car parked near the detached garage, and Anton chopping wood in the front yard. Judging by the pile of split wood beside him and the sweat soaking his undershirt, he'd been there a while.

"Look at that," Sergei greeted him after he parked. "Almost like a respectable man, I'm impressed."

Anton swung the axe down, leaving it embedded in the stump he'd been using as a chopping block. "My grandfather taught me before he died. It's therapeutic."

"No wonder you were so good at cracking skulls," Sergei said.

His words elicited a subtle shift in the younger man, his spine straightening to form a rigid line down the center of his back as he squared his shoulders. "That's not all I'm good at," he replied defensively, facing off against Sergei directly. "Your old man could see my potential, why can't you?"

"I see it," he said. Picking up Anton's shirt from the edge of the wood pile, he held it out to him. "That's not the problem I have with you."

"Then what is?" Anton demanded but his countenance was already shifting. Accepting his shirt, he pulled it on loosely.

"The same as it's always been," Sergei answered. "You have potential but you squander it. You behave wantonly and you're dissolute."

"If I'm dissolute it's because I haven't got anything to do," the younger man protested. "Give me something important to manage!"

"Something important, for you to manage?" Sergei gave a pained laugh. "Do you know something, Anton? You can't manage to keep yourself out of a bottle for more than twenty-four hours. Do you think I'm an idiot?"

"Then if I stop, you'll give me something to do?" he asked. "Something serious?"

"Oy, oy, oy," Sergei exclaimed. "Here we go again. How many times have you said you'd clean up? Huh?" He waited for an answer but received only sullen-faced resentment. "Speak up, surely you kept count. It must be at least a dozen times. At least! And you want to manage something important?"

Anton was avoiding his eyes now, the line of his back softened as his shoulders slumped. Sergei could only shake his head. The man in front of him had been little more than a teenage gangster when his father passed by and scraped him out of the gutter.

Pasha and Dima had joined the family as boys, and being roughly the same age as Sergei they'd all bonded well. But Anton was different, a teenage street punk eight years younger than any of them, with no remaining family to speak of and a budding criminal career to show for it.

He was ruthless and wild, a thief even from those who fed him, well on his way to a life spent in and out of criminal institutions. It was no wonder that Sergei's father, seeing in the teen boy a reflection of himself at that age, had felt an affinity for the dispossessed youth and brought him home.

To say Anton hadn't integrated well into the established family order would be putting it lightly. His innate competitiveness, mixed with an overwhelming desire to win their father's approval, became the source of endless tension and fights during the early years. At times he tried to stir up rivalry between the brothers, particularly Pasha and Dima. The results invariably backfired on him and eventually the newcomer realized that he would have to adapt if he wanted to be accepted.

Almost ten years later, that adaptation was still a work in progress.

"I'd do it if you ever gave me something meaningful to do," Anton insisted. "I haven't had a decent job since the old man died."

Anton's transition from calling Sergei's father dad to the old man had happened in the aftermath of his death. Taking it for a coping mechanism to distance himself from the grief of losing his closest friend, mentor, and paternal figure, the older men had chosen not to comment on the change.

"If you're serious about it this time, you're in luck," Sergei informed him. "Come inside and get cleaned up, I'll explain why I called you."

The last time Anton saw Lila Sverlova, they were attending his father's funeral. Vasily Ivanov had been more than a surrogate father to Anton–he was a savior. In Vasily's care, he'd felt safe. Secure. For the first time in years, no one could taunt or torment him, no one could abuse him and get away with it. It was like a balm for his damaged soul, and though his progress was slow, he began to mend, to become once again more human than beast.

Along with a new family–a mother and father, three older brothers, and an older sister to be found in Olga–Anton gained an uncle in Yuriy. Like Vasily, Yuriy felt a certain fellowship with the misguided teenager, and Anton often spent holidays with the Sverlovs.

One summer would stay in his memory forever, though. It was the summer of his eighteenth birthday, when he received his first car as a gift from Vasily and promptly drove cross-country to the Baikal in order to join Yuriy's family for a month of swimming, hiking, and fishing at their cabin on the lake.

Of course Lila was there too, enjoying a brief hiatus before her final year at the finishing school, all long-limbed and smooth-skinned. It wasn't the first time they'd spent the summer together, but it was the first time he saw her as a woman and there'd been no going back.

Similarly, there was no going back now that he stood before the door of her apartment with a bouquet of flowers in one hand and a box of chocolates in the other. If there was a god, in Anton's view he was immeasurably cruel.

"Who is it?" an unfamiliar voice asked through the door.

"Is Lila home?" Anton asked.

There was a moment of silence, followed by the sound of the door being unbolted and a moment later it swung open to reveal a slender young brunette.

"She's in the shower," the woman said, leaning in the doorway to look him over appraisingly. "And who are you?"

"Her cousin," Anton lied, sidestepping the woman to enter the apartment. Removing his shoes, he continued toward the kitchen.

"Ooh, I see," the woman said. Closing the door, she followed him down the narrow hall. "I didn't know she had such a handsome cousin. I'm Lidia, by the way."

"Mmhm," he responded, disinterested in her chatter. "Our Lila is from a large and loving family, she's an aunt too if you can believe it."

Setting the flowers and chocolate on the kitchen table, he turned back to Lidia. "And now, do you have a reason to be here?"

Her eyes widened in surprise and uncertainty. "We were just hanging out. Why?"

"Then I think it's time for you to go," he said, staring at her meaningfully. "Forgive my rudeness but we need to speak privately. I'm afraid I come bearing bad news. It's a family matter; I'm sure you understand."

"Oh, I'm so sorry," she said. "Yes, of course. I'll just get my coat, could you tell Lila I'll see her on Monday?"

"Yes, thank you," Anton replied. Seeing her out, he closed the double doors behind her and returned to the kitchen to wait.

Waiting gave him time to think. Even before the funeral, his contact with Lila had grown sporadic. After she turned eighteen, everything seemed to change. Or maybe he just hadn't wanted to see what was right in front of him all along.

When Sergei returned from studying in America, Anton's friendship with Lila waned as she oriented herself toward the expected marriage to the hero of her romantic fantasies. And why not? By that point, Sergei was a grown man in his late twenties, possessing the confidence of someone with enough sexual experience to seduce any woman he wanted. He ran important branches of the family business, vacationed with his brothers in the most exclusive resorts, and traveled abroad to study foreign markets.

As if to add insult atop injury, Sergei was a classically handsome man. Tall, strong, a natural athlete who excelled in common sports. Rumor had it that the Ivanov's descended from Russian aristocracy and it only took one good look at Sergei to see why. If it was true, the family had fallen far from grace, but that didn't change anything. Anton knew he couldn't compete.

"Lidia?" The shower had stopped and Lila called for her friend.

"She left," Anton called back, rising from the chair to lean in the hallway near the bathroom door. During one of his more disastrous attempts at integrating with society, wherein he tried attending school in the city for a year, he'd stayed regularly at her apartment. He remembered it well.

"Anton?" she sounded understandably surprised.

"Yes, it's me," he answered. "I brought you some presents. I'll wait in the kitchen."

"Wait!" He could hear her fumbling in the bathroom for a moment before the door was flung open. "What the hell are you doing here, how'd you get in?"

Lila's face glowed from her recent shower, framed by the wet strands of her hair as they curled around her chin. She'd wrapped a thin towel around her torso, beads of water clinging to her skin as she stared at him. Full and soft, her breasts were pressed together by the tight wrap of the towel, straining against the fabric. Instant erection material.

Anton breathed in sharply, struggling to tear his heated gaze away from her.

"Your friend let me in," he answered.

"I'm sure she did," Lila said, eyes sweeping over him. "Why are you here?"

"Get dressed first," he suggested. "I'll tell you in the kitchen."

For a moment it looked like she might protest but with a huff that expanded her ample cleavage and threatened to dislodge her towel in the process, she turned and hurried down the hall. Anton remained where he was, waiting until the door closed behind her before he returned to the kitchen.

A few minutes later, Lila emerged wearing a set of loose-fitting pajamas and tugging a comb through her wet hair. Once she was satisfied with her hair, she tossed the comb aside and went to the fridge for a glass of orange juice. Finally, glass of juice in hand, she settled into a chair on the opposite side of the table from Anton.

"You can put the flowers in water," she said, staring at him over the bouquet of lilacs and daisies. "What's the occasion? Must be important for you to show up with flowers in hand but not a call or text ahead."

Picking up the box of chocolates, she ran a nail under the seal and popped the top off to peruse its contents. Anton didn't comment, opting instead to pick out a vase from the cupboard over the stove.

Adding a teaspoon of sugar to the water, he unwrapped the bouquet and set it on the cutting board. Using a chef's knife from the block on the counter, he trimmed two inches from the stems, swept the unwanted plant matter into the trash, and then arranged the bouquet in the vase.

"My lady," he said, turning back to Lila to present the vase.

"On the table is fine," she said dismissively. "Why did Sergei send you?"

Anton bristled at his brother's name. "What makes you assume he did?"

His question earned a derisive snort from her. "Lilacs and daisies with a box of gold-foil chocolates from Le Petit Chien? This has been Sergei's gift to me since I was five." She shook her head. "It's fine, clearly you didn't know. Even if you hadn't brought his gift, I'd still have known Sergei sent you."

With a long-suffering sigh, Anton took his seat again, sinking back to look at her as she savored one of the chocolates from her box. "Why?"

"Because of the timing," she said. "I haven't seen you since the funeral, and that was almost a year ago. But my father has been AWOL for a few weeks now, and I can imagine how that might be a concern for Sergei. You know he likes to avoid making a scene, and he knows I still have a bone to pick with him, but I have no such bone with you. So it's only logical he'd pick you to approach me. The extra bribery is a nice touch, he knows what I love. Do you want one?" She offered the box of chocolates to Anton.

"I'd rather have something to drink," he replied but took one at random anyway.

"You can forget about that," Lila laughed. "I don't supply free booze to alcoholics."

"I'm not an alcoholic," he said, bristling at her comment. "I just like to drink. You would too given my position."

"Yes, keep telling yourself that," she encouraged sarcastically. "Because denial has gotten you so far already."

"You know what? Fuck you," he swore, rising from his seat.

"Sit down!" Lila ordered, freezing him in his place. "I didn't say you could leave. You barged in, ran off my friend, and ruined my plans for the evening. The least you can do is sit down and tell me what Sergei wants."

"Ask him yourself," he said. He didn't leave, but he didn't sit either, standing by the table and looking down at Lila as she glared at him.

After a minute of stiff silence, her gaze softened and she finally asked, "Anton, what happened to you?"

CHAPTER XII

Loyalty

The following day, Lila arrived at just past one o'clock in the afternoon, driving up in her powder-blue BMW. Sergei was waiting when she arrived, neatly dressed in a casual, slate-gray suit. You'd have to know him to realize he was dressed for business. In contrast, she'd poured her generous figure into a bandage dress that clung to each curve like a second skin, and her hair bounced around her shoulders in a mass of perfectly formed curls. Apparently she was intent on showing him just what he'd missed out on by turning her down.

Sergei was unfazed by Lila's provocative choice of clothes, not least of all because thoughts of Eleanor kept encroaching on him.

"Lila," he greeted her with a warm kiss on the back of each hand. "You look as lovely as ever."

"Seryozha," she replied, surprisingly demure. "I received your peace offering. As I already told Anton, I doubt there's anything I'm going to be able to say that helps you deal with my father, but I'm here anyway. Shall we?"

Inside, they settled in the small dining room off the kitchen rather than the more grandiose dining hall. The table was already laid, with plate warmers keeping the food hot. Pouring out a shot of vodka for himself, Sergei took a seat opposite Lila.

78

"I know you're not an idiot," he began, "so I'm not going to treat you like one. You don't have any idea where your father is hiding?"

"That's what I told Anton," she confirmed, meeting his eyes without a flicker of hesitation. "Dad mentioned some things to me, I know you two have been quietly feuding since Uncle Vasya died."

"You know no small part of that feuding stems from my refusal to marry you," Sergei stated flatly.

"Yes, well–" she looked away "–I can't help that, can I? I'm not the one who had a problem with the idea."

Sergei knew a pointless argument was brewing but he hadn't asked her there to argue about their romantic past, or lack thereof. "Do you seriously think I'll believe he left you without any way to get in touch? What if you needed something?"

Lila shrugged. "I don't really care what you believe, Sergei. I'm pretty good at taking care of myself these days, I have an apartment, the bills are paid, there is food. And plenty of money. What else do I need?"

She was lying when she said she didn't care what he thought, Sergei didn't need to have known her from the day she was born to realize that. He couldn't tell if she was being truthful about the rest, though. Lila had inherited no small part of her father's sense of pride, and hers had been badly wounded by his rejection. Even if she was struggling, she might not tell him.

"It's not like him, Lila," he argued, running a hand through his hair in agitation. "Yuriy loves you more than anyone else. You're his favorite. He must have left you a number, an email address. What is it?"

"I think you must have forgotten how stubborn my father can be," she informed him.

"I haven't forgotten." He ground his teeth together, jaw clenching. "If he wasn't so stubborn we wouldn't be in this situation."

Lila shook her head. "You're just as stubborn."

"I'm not," he disagreed. "Lila, he's your father, tell me where he is, or at least give me a number. You know I won't hurt him but I need to speak to him, this feud must be resolved before it leads to blood."

She regarded him with a cool expression, then just shook her head again but this time is was more sad than negative. "I can't tell you what I don't know."

"You must know!"

"I don't!" she insisted vehemently. Her cool expression changed, flashing quickly through sadness to frustration and she burst out, "I haven't heard anything from him since he left, I don't know where he went or when he'll come home because I took your side when you two started fighting."

The admission was accompanied by a burst of uncontrollable tears as she continued, "and just because I took your side doesn't mean I don't miss my father or worry about where he's gone. We hadn't talked for weeks before he left. So there, are you happy? The house is sitting empty, and my sisters won't talk to me either."

"Your sisters won't talk to you?" Sergei echoed her words. Lila nodded. "Why not?"

"Galya is too busy with her husband and the new baby, we've barely talked since Sonya was born," Lila explained, speaking of her oldest sister, Galina.

"And Valentina?"

"Took dad's side, of course," she answered. "Now she might know where he went, but she won't tell you."

That was true. Of the three sisters, Valentina had always been the prim and proper one. She took after their deceased mother, a woman who had been equal parts vain and proud, and who had gone to her grave believing she descended from an old aristocratic family. Valentina inherited that belief, and like her mother she possessed a certain disdain for criminal activities. The fact that her own family's wealth, her father's very status and prestige, stemmed from strictly criminal pursuits somehow went unnoticed by Valentina as she entertained the notion that she was a refined lady of noble birth and inherent grace.

"No, she won't talk," Sergei grumbled, more to himself than to Lila. "But she might tell you."

"I doubt it," Lila said. "The last time we talked, she called me a simpleminded idiot who would hang out her father just to please the boy she likes."

"Oy," Sergei sighed. "I'm sorry, Lilochka."

"It's fine," she said, waving her hand dismissively. "Why be upset if it's the truth? But no, she won't tell me. The last time we talked was weeks ago, just after dad left. Don't think I've just been waiting around to hear from you. I care about my dad."

"I know," he said. There were good reasons why Lila was Yuriy's favorite, not least of which was the fact that she was the youngest. When her older sisters began chasing after boyfriends and then getting married, Lila had long declared that she would stay with their father in the family home forever. How she reconciled that notion with her fantasies of marrying him, Sergei had never understood. Perhaps she thought he would move in?

Sergei shook his head at the thought. Another of the many reasons why he would never, ever marry Lila. Not in a million years.

It took two more days of working on the case, but then Eleanor had an epiphany. After getting her hands on a map of the local region, she'd marked out the places where each victim's body was found. At first there didn't seem to be any pattern. No matter which way she turned the map, she couldn't figure out how the points were connected–but they had to be.

Frustrated and tired of making no progress, she left her work on the table and decided to take a shower in the hope of relaxing her mind. As it turned out, it was exactly what she needed. With hot water flowing over her head, she began going over all the details of the case again in her head. Ages, genders, locations of the bodies, she'd been looking for some common detail that tied them all together and then it occurred to her.

They had all been ritually silenced.

With her thoughts rushing ahead of her, she hurried to rinse off and grabbed a towel. Still only half-dry, she retrieved her phone to call Sergei.

"*Da, privet,*" he answered after the second ring.

"Sergei? It's me," she said. "Do you have time to talk?"

"Now?" He paused. "What is it?"

"I have some questions about the case," she explained. "Do you think you could come to the hotel for dinner?"

The line was silent for a moment before he answered. "Yes, I can be there in two hours. Will that do?"

"Yes, please come straight up when you get here," she said. "And Sergei?"

"*Da?*"

"Drive carefully." She wanted to say I love you but bit her tongue. "I'll see you soon."

"Of course," he affirmed. "*Poka.*"

With that, the call ended. Setting her phone aside, Eleanor let out a breath she hadn't realized she was holding. There was a strange feeling of disappointment in the center of her breast. What had she expected to hear when she called him, romantic poetry? Confessions of love? She shook her head, such notions were foolish. Who knew where he was or who he was with, of course he wasn't going to wax romantic over the phone.

Opting to make the time pass as quickly as possible, Eleanor finished drying off and got dressed, then set about to combing the tangles from her hair. Rather than leave it loose to dry, she twisted it into a braid, tying it off expertly with an elastic. Usually it was Ana's hair that she braided, two long pigtails that already reached her waist. Opening her email, she pulled up the most recent photos her mother had sent.

As a surprise to distract her from Eleanor's absence, her mother had taken Ana to the Oregon Coast Aquarium for two days. Her email was full of pictures of her daughter, grinning broadly and waving wildly to the camera as they watched penguins and puffins, then sea lions, otters, and an endless array of crustaceans and other, more exotic invertebrates.

'Tomorrow we have a whale watching tour across the bay so she can see the seals on the buoys and the orca pod if it's in the area. Rented that cottage on the ocean where dad used to take you. She loves it, and your old scribbles on the wall behind the radiator are still there. Someday they'll be painted over but for now your mark on history remains.' With promises of more pictures the following day, the email was lovingly signed from Ana and Grandma. Flipping through the pictures for a few more minutes, she finally closed her email and leaned back in her seat. She'd been in Russia for a week already, half the allotted time on her entry visa, but it felt like barely a day or two had passed.

Her departing flight was in eight days. She stared at the ticket sitting on the table next to her laptop, wishing she'd arranged to be in the country longer. But how could she? If Kossakov's killer took her longer than two weeks to profile, he'd already confirmed she could take the work back to the States to continue. And she had to return, Ana was waiting with all the patience a six-year-old could muster. She'd circled the date of her flight home on the calendar so that the little blonde imp could count down the days, certain of her return.

Still, after finally having found Sergei, after being with him again, her heart protested. It protested against the fact she had to leave, and it protested against her silence about Ana. She longed to ask him to return with her, to come to America and meet his daughter. In her mind, she could already see the look on Ana's face when she would be introduced to her father. To meet her father was the wish she made every year when she blew out her birthday candles, and when everyone in her kindergarten class wrote letters to Santa, Ana's letter begged him not to give her any presents ever again if only he could bring her father back instead.

What sort of mother was she to deny her daughter's most ardent wish? I can't tell him, I can't, I can't, she repeated the thought like a mantra. Sergei was a criminal, and she still didn't know what he'd done or what he might be willing to do. When she thought about it in the broad light of day, those facts didn't seem so hedonistically arousing anymore–they sent a cold chill down her spine. Ana was too precious for her to take chances.

Glancing to the clock, she realized it was almost time for him to arrive and rose, hurrying to the bathroom to rinse her face. Her eyes were slightly bloodshot but if Sergei noticed, she'd simply put it down to lack of sleep. Which was true enough–profiling the murderer had kept her up through most of the previous night. The case tied her mind (not to mention her stomach) in knots until she realized what was the most probable connection. And it'd been staring her in the face: the simplest solution is usually the correct one.

From the window she watched for Sergei to arrive. She didn't have to wait long before he pulled up close to the curb and handed off his keys to the valet before disappearing from view when he entered the hotel. It didn't take long for him to reach her room. Letting the door swing open before he had a chance to knock, she ushered him in.

CHAPTER XIII

Acquiesce

The door clicked shut behind him as Sergei swept her into his arms, bundling her close against his chest and raising her lips to his. He kissed her intensely, cradling her face between his hands as their breaths mingled.

"Mm, I missed you too," she whispered huskily, reaching down automatically to grip his belt and pull him closer. "Thank you for coming. Shall we order room service now? I haven't eaten."

"By all means," he agreed, stepping out of his shoes and following her to the table. He took the phone from her, asking, "what do you want?"

"I hadn't decided," Eleanor shrugged, taking a seat on the miniature couch as she regarded him. "Order for me, you know what I like."

Sergei returned her comment with a smoldering look that spoke volumes. Dialing the extension for room service, he waited for a minute and then greeted someone in Russian. After a brief exchange that Eleanor didn't understand in the slightest, he thanked the person on the other end of the line and set the phone back in its cradle.

"It is done," he informed her, pulling out one of the chairs tucked under the small table in order to take a seat in front of her. "They'll bring dinner in twenty minutes.

"Now tell me, what did you need to talk to me about?"

"It's your sister's case. I think the killer is performing a ritual of silencing," she explained. "It's a disgusting old occult ritual that practitioners of so-called black magic have written about."

"What does he need a ritual for? Murdering his victims silenced them rather effectively if you ask me," Sergei pointed out.

"I don't think he was trying to silence his victims, per se," Eleanor began, shifting uncomfortably in her spot.

"Then who?" he asked.

"I think he's trying to silence the families of the victims, to curse them with ruin," she said. "I know it sounds nuts, because it is, but that's what I need to ask you about. Who are the other people that he killed? Do you know any of them?"

He regarded her quietly for a moment, and Eleanor worried that he might scoff at her statement or treat her theory with disdain. Instead, a disturbed expression grew in his eyes, and after a long moment he exhaled his breath.

"Do you have their pictures?" he asked.

Nodding, she stood and retrieved the file Kossakov had given her. Resuming her seat, she flipped the file open to withdraw a thin stack of photographs. Sergei's older sister, Olga, was pictured at the top of the pile.

"Here," she offered, holding out the pictures. She watched closely as Sergei began looking through the photos, keen to gauge any reaction he might have, however subtle. If her theory held true, the thread that connected the murders was one of criminality. The victims must have been connected, in some way or another, to the thieves' world. She could feel it in her gut.

"*Nu da*," Sergei sighed, nodding as he flipped through the photographs. Each person's name and date of birth was written on the back of their photo. When he was finished, he handed her four photos. "I know these ones."

"The others?" she asked hopefully.

"*Nyet*," he stated firmly, shaking his head, "but that doesn't mean anything, it's not as if I have a database in my head. I'll have someone look into the rest. These ones, though–" he indicated the four pictures "–I know their families."

Eleanor looked at the pictures. Natasha Cherkova, Arkady Semenov, Tula Lemonova, and Nikita Sokolov.

"And they were involved in criminal activities?"

"It depends on who you ask," he said. "Cherkhova's father ran a small-time smuggling ring until he died; tax-free imports from abroad, counterfeit cigarettes, spirits, and cigars that they ran over the borders in Poland, Ukraine, Lithuania. Her brothers took over the family business, she went to the city to attend school. She was good, but her brothers are scum."

"The others?" she asked.

"Sokolov was an old timer, my father was acquainted with him years ago. Collections, security, intimidation. He's old in this picture, he was much stronger when he was young; people respected him," Sergei said. "Lemonova worked in a salon and had a drug problem. Her brother is a petty dealer."

That only left Arkady Semenov.

"That one was an arms dealer," he said, pointing at the young man. "Mostly old war trophies, some modern equipment from Germany and Israel. Junk he bought cheap and resold to vengeful idiots."

Eleanor raised an eyebrow at that. "Why wasn't any of this information in the file?"

Sergei simply shrugged. "Put anyone under a microscope in this country and you're going to find some shit on them. Everyone has secrets." He cast her a pointed look.

"Indeed," she sighed, pressing her lips into a thin line of dissatisfaction. "Well these people are all dead, so unless you want them to take their secrets to the grave, I need to know everything that might connect their murders. How quickly can you get the remaining cases checked out?"

He glanced at his watch, then picked up the paperwork on the four remaining victims and flipped through it briefly. Arranging their biography papers in a square on the table, he snapped a picture with his cell phone and then tapped swiftly across the screen, entering a message to someone.

"They'll be checked. We'll know whether you're right within a day, maybe two," he informed her a moment later.

His entire demeanor, from the look in his eyes to the tone of his voice, was so assured and relaxed about the matter–clearly it wasn't the first time he'd put a trace on someone. Eleanor watched him, wondering what had turned him into such a hardened criminal. A knock on the door interrupted her thoughts, and a waiter from the kitchen delivered their meal. Taking over at the door, Sergei pressed a tip into the man's hand and wheeled the trolley into the room, letting the door swing shut behind him.

"Is there anything else to discuss before we eat?" he asked.

"No. I have some thoughts, but it's just conjecture until we hear back about the other victims," she said.

"*Khorosho, davai,*" he said, arranging their food. "Let's eat."

He'd ordered a bottle of white wine to go with their meal, and poured generously. "To you," he intoned, raising his glass.

"I'll drink to that," she agreed, lifting her own but pausing before their glasses touched. "And to you."

"Indeed." They clinked and drank in unison, then settled in to enjoy the meal. Whatever he'd ordered was good, she didn't know the name of the dish, and thankfully there wasn't a layer of fresh dill over everything. Savory pieces of meat melted in her mouth, followed by exquisitely spiced fingerling potatoes and a wash of the wine. It was a mouthwatering combination but her attention was fixed more on Sergei than the food.

Perhaps it was simply that his mannerisms had changed with the years, but something seemed different. She watched him as they ate, wondering what thoughts hid behind those enigmatic blue eyes. Apparently her patience was to be rewarded. Upon finishing his meal, he leaned back, relaxing for a moment before pouring out the rest of the wine into her glass. From the feeling of lightheaded drunkenness that clouded her thoughts, Eleanor had enough sense to suspect that she'd drunk most of the bottle.

"For what reason have you plied me so heavily with wine?" she asked, looking from her half-full glass to the empty bottle and then back to him. The corner of his mouth lifted in a fleeting grin.

"Perhaps I want to seduce you again," he suggested.

"Mm, I don't think so," she sighed, leaning back into the small couch. "You've never needed alcohol to seduce me and you know it."

"*Nu da, ya znayu,*" he agreed.

"So are you going to tell me?" she asked. "Or will I die of suspense?"

"Maybe," he said, regarding her with a darkened gaze. "Will you promise not to protest?"

Eleanor regarded him as seriously as she could, struggling to maintain a steady train of thought with the alcohol so thoroughly saturating her blood. It wasn't that the wine had been particularly strong, but she was a relative lightweight and two-thirds of a bottle was enough to render her quite drunk. Even so, his request roused her suspicion.

"Why, is it something kinky?" she asked before thinking twice and was taken aback by Sergei's bark of laughter.

"Would you consent if it was?" he returned suggestively. "I think you would. But no, my filthy-minded little Amerikanachka, it isn't kinky."

"Then dispense with the suspense and tell me," she suggested.

"First promise me you won't protest."

Her hesitation was short-lived. "As you wish, I won't protest."

"Come with me to the countryside," he said, raising a hand to silence her before her mouth even opened. "You just promised not to protest."

"That doesn't mean I won't decline," she said, shaking her head. "Sergei, do you even hear what you're talking about? I have to work on the case, and I leave in a week."

"I know," he said. "That's why I want you to come with me now. There's internet at the dacha and it's only a couple hours drive from the city. You can bring your things, I'll take you to the airport the day of your flight."

Eleanor shifted in her seat, not uncomfortable so much as uneasy about Sergei's suggestion. Moscow was a major city, all things considered. Despite Russia's reputation for being a wild, lawless country, she felt safe in the city, and could communicate with the English-speaking hotel staff in case of need. A several hour drive into the countryside with a known criminal, no matter if he was her lover, rang alarm bells even in her wine-fogged brain.

"I don't know," she began, shaking her head. That was a bad idea, making her head spin from the alcohol.

"The lady doth protest too much. Come with me," he persisted.

"I can't," she insisted, but her resolve was weak. Through the haze that clouded her mind, she realized he was going to win, and not just because he'd loosened her up with alcohol. If the dacha was the same one that he'd told her about before, truth was that she wanted to see it. Badly. Somehow, she felt that if she could see the place Sergei had grown up as a child, it would tell her more about him, perhaps bring them closer together. His descriptions made it sound like paradise, a stretch of idyllic countryside on the outskirts of a rural village where his grandmother raised her own ducks, kept a henhouse, and always fattened a pig each year to feed family and friends through winter. It didn't make sense to her that someone could grow up in such ideal circumstances, only to become a brazen criminal as an adult.

Perhaps brazen was too strong a term. In fact, so far Eleanor had failed to identify much of anything that would have given Sergei away to the average eye. If not for his tattoos and the forced, de facto confession that she'd extracted from him, she probably wouldn't have suspected him to be involved in anything untoward. The man was simply too smooth, too polished and refined, to think he would be associated with the criminal world. It made her wonder even more–what exactly had he done to earn such tattoos?

And what did he do now? Searching for his sister's killer was all well and good, but a desire for vengeance didn't indicate much about his life. Come to think of it, his thirst for blood indicated that the man she so romanticized was fully prepared to carry out his own extrajudicial killing. All these things ran through her head, a disjointed array of muddled thoughts and confusion, but through it all a thread of curiosity held her, entangled with Sergei and his sister's case and her own hopeless attraction to the man sitting so calmly before her, close enough for their knees to nearly brush.

"Why?" she finally asked.

"Because I promised to show you the dacha," he answered. "I want to keep my promise, and I want to show you my homeland."

"But I'm already here, seeing it," she said. "And I need to work."

"*Nyet,*" he said firmly. "You won't find the heart of Russia here, in the city."

"Then where?" she asked.

"In the countryside," he said. "Come with me, Nora. The house is waiting, there's bound to be fruit in the garden. Let me finally keep my promise."

It was an old promise, seven years old to be precise. Softened by his insistence, and driven by no small curiosity of her own, Eleanor agreed.

CHAPTER XIV

Motherland

Eleanor awoke to a fine headache and the sound of birdsong early the next morning. Disoriented and groggy from the prior evening's indulgence, she sat up slowly and rubbed her eyes. Bright light shone through the sheer curtains that covered a window to her right, and Sergei was stretched beside her on a narrow bed, still asleep. With a groan, she turned and buried her head in the pillow. Oh this is just great, she commended herself with no small touch of sarcasm. Get drunk, leave the city, and wind up in bed with him again only God knows where...

All she remembered was a long drive down dark roads, nodding in and out of sleep before they arrived somewhere at the end of a gravel drive. She sighed heavily, willing the steadily pulsing pain in her head to go away so she could think clearly. Beside her, she felt Sergei shifting and opened her eyes to find him stretched on his side, watching her.

"*Dobroye utro,*" he greeted her.

"I assume that means good morning?"

"*Da,*" he nodded, wrapping an arm around her waist to pull her closer. Not that there'd been much distance between them anyway, but now she could feel the hot press of his skin flush against hers, separated only by the thin fabric of her tank top. He pressed a kiss to her forehead. "How do you feel?"

"Like a lightweight who drank way too much," she answered grouchily. "Where on earth did you bring me?"

"Och, my sleeping beauty awakens," he said. "Don't start protesting, you already agreed so it's too late. We're at the dacha, as promised. Your things are in the living room."

"Of course," she sighed, closing her eyes in a futile attempt to escape the bright light that was aggravating her headache. "Do you have any painkillers?"

"*Da*, stay here and I'll get you something," he instructed, sliding out from between the sheets.

When he returned several minutes later, Sergei was carrying a lidded tea cup and saucer. Sitting up, she accepted the cup and waited expectantly for him to produce some form of over-the-counter pain killer. Instead, her boxer-clad lover took a seat on the edge of the bed and prompted her to sip the hot liquid. Removing the lid, she was met with the strong aroma of mint mixed with honey and recoiled slightly.

"Mint tea?" she asked doubtfully. "Don't you have something else?"

"Less face making, more drinking," he replied. "This will cure your headache and is better than any pill."

Eleanor made a face. "You may not be aware of this, but I am not especially fond of mint. I don't even like it in my toothpaste."

"Drink," he insisted. "This is local peppermint with willow extract and raw honey from the wild bees. It's a remedy over a thousand years old. You'll feel better by the time you're done."

Recognizing the futility of arguing with him over the matter, she held her breath and took a tentative sip from the edge of the cup. It was hot but not scalding, and the taste of mint wasn't quite as overwhelming as she anticipated. The honey was flavorful, with just the right level of sweetness, and there was a slightly tangy aftertaste that mixed with the minty coolness. Shaking her head as a shiver ran down her spine, she made a face.

"Bleh, minty," she announced, holding the cup away for a moment before taking another sip. She cast Sergei an accusatory glare. "I think you like making me suffer. Where did you come up with this concoction?"

"It's a local remedy," he answered. "Every family has their own variation. I could add some lemon if you prefer."

"No, it's fine," she declined. "I'll just stomach it the way it is."

"The taste grows on you," he assured her. "And it's good for upset stomachs or when you get sick. Drink, drink," he encouraged. "I'll bring you something to eat. The bathroom's through that door–" he pointed to a door that was half-hidden behind a large wardrobe on the other side of the room "–I'll be right back."

The countryside was something else alright. From the moment she stepped out into the mid-morning sunshine and inhaled her first breath of the clean, crisp air, Eleanor felt her lingering regret about agreeing melt away. After stomaching the entire cup of Sergei's shamanistic brew masquerading itself as tea, she had to admit that she felt markedly better. The fresh bread and cheese he'd offered her helped too, but best of all had been the perfectly crisp croissants. Where he'd managed to obtain such delicacies was a mystery, they were nowhere near a pastry shop or any other hallmark of modern civilization, but she wasn't about to complain.

"Where did you get these?" she asked, munching away and enjoying each bite of the flaky delight. "I didn't even know Russians made croissants."

"We looted the recipe when we beat Napoleon," he replied. Apparently he was rather pleased at having absconded from the city with her, because his good mood only seemed to get better and was starting to feel slightly contagious. For the life of her, Eleanor couldn't summon the urge to be cross with him. Instead, she was curious. She couldn't wait to look around the area.

"I don't hear any ducks," she commented, peering out at the yard as she got her first glimpse of the Russian countryside. Tall trees and gently rolling hills obscured the distant road and any other signs of external civilization. Eleanor didn't see any other houses either, though there was an older outbuilding not far from the front porch. From the look of the peeling paint and discolored wood, it had weathered some years of negligent ownership.

"The flock moved into the village after babushka died," Sergei said, joining her for a leisurely walk around the house. Large, mostly-flat rocks had been set around the perimeter of the house to form a walkway. The stepping stones had been recently cleared of weeds, and led to the back garden and fenced area with an abandoned chicken coop that was heavily overgrown with weeds. Whatever was planted in the garden was wildly overgrown too, with flowers and some persistent vegetables tangled up in a mess of weeds. Hidden behind the overgrowth of the garden was a pond with reeds and water grass growing around the perimeter.

"I guess no one else in the family likes to garden, huh?" she observed, taking in the garden's poor state.

Sergei shrugged, taking a few steps away from the stones.

"*Nu da,*" he agreed. "It's been over ten years since she died. We could have maintained it better but when you're in Moscow, sometimes it feels like everything else is a world away."

"That's a shame, I'd love to have a place like this," Eleanor said, stepping off the stones to walk around the garden plot. "Who is 'we'?"

"Who?" Sergei looked at her.

"You said 'we' could have maintained it better," she said. "Who did you mean?"

"My brothers," he answered.

"I thought Olga was your only sibling," she said in surprise.

"My only sister," he confirmed. "I also have three brothers."

Eleanor's eyebrows rose halfway up her head as she looked at him. Did she hear that right? "You have three brothers?"

"*Da.*" Sergei nodded, apparently unfazed by her surprise. "Pavel, Dimitri, and our youngest brother, Anton."

"I thought your mom was in her seventies now," she said.

"She is," he confirmed. "My brothers were adopted. Pasha, Dima, and I grew up together from the time we were boys. Dad adopted Anton last, years ago."

"Strange," Eleanor said. "You never mentioned them."

He shrugged, reaching out to snap a stalk of horsetail in half. "I suppose it didn't seem necessary at the time."

His answer was a far cry from satisfactory, but she was inclined to let it pass for the time being. At least he was willing to tell her now. While they were on the subject, she asked, "do you have any other family?"

"After a fashion," he answered, but didn't elaborate. He continued his assault on the patch of horsetail, snapping the stalks with a vengeance. Eleanor sighed, shaking her head.

"You'll never get rid of them that way," she commented. "They grow back home, too-invasive menace. You've got to get at the roots, dig them out and don't give them a chance to spread their spores. Otherwise you'll just be doing this forever."

"*Da,*" he agreed. "We used to burn the field and bury it with brush each fall to prepare for spring planting. My babushka's tradition, but as you can see it's one we've failed to keep up with."

"That's a shame," Eleanor said. She meant it, but new questions were brewing in her mind. "Tell me about your brothers. Are they like you?"

"In what way?" Sergei seemed to intentionally beat around the bush.

"*Vor,*" she said, using the Russian term for a thief.

Regarding her silently, he shook his head, reaching up to run a hand loosely through his hair. "In a word, yes. But when is life ever so simple?" he asked.

Looking out across the garden, he continued, "Pasha and Dima are two of the finest men I've ever known. We've been through some dark things together, shed blood for one another. You can't judge them, my law-abiding little Amerikanachka. You don't know what sort of filth they came from."

"True enough," she admitted. "So tell me about them. You seem close, do you all stay in contact?"

"You could say that," he answered. The shadow of a smile caught the corner of his mouth, sunshine illuminating his blue eyes brilliantly as he looked over the countryside with obvious fondness. "We spent so many summers here. Look–" he took her hand, drawing her with him past the garden to a stand of fruit trees nearly hidden by the tall grass. Stomping a path through the grass and weeds, he reached for a low-hanging branch and presented it to Eleanor.

"You came at just the right time," he said, watching as she plucked several bright red fruit from the branch. "The first cherries of the season."

Unsure if he was avoiding the topic or just enthusiastic about the countryside, Eleanor tried again. "Do you want to tell me about your brothers?"

"*Da nyet, ne znayu,*" he answered. "Oy, looks like the blueberries survived too."

Popping a cherry into her mouth and enjoying the burst of sweetness with a touch of tartness, she watched Sergei as he enthusiastically assaulted a huge blueberry bush. It looked every bit as wild as the rest of the miniature orchard and garden, surrounded by a thick overgrowth of weeds and grass. She'd never seen such an enormous bush, and upon closer inspection she realized that there were actually two large, mature plants tangled up with several younger bushes, wild starters that must have cropped up from the uncollected berries of years past. He returned victorious, with a handful of the succulent berries. Each blueberry was easily the size of a marble, and they ranged in color from dark blue and purple to nearly black. Presenting his open palm to her, he picked out a berry and held it to her in offering.

Accepting it, she felt his fingertips graze over her mouth. The contact sent blood rushing to her lips and a jolt down her spine. However intoxicating his touch and delicious the fruit, though, it wasn't enough to distract her from his guarded avoidance of her query. And she couldn't help her curiosity, now that she knew he had additional family, she wanted to know more. After all, if they were his family, then they were Ana's family too. It made for a small world when your only known relatives were mom and grandma–it was nice to think she might have more family on her father's side.

Except for the part about being criminals. Eleanor bit her tongue, lost in the intensity of his gaze and uncertain what else to say. The last thing she wanted was to nag him; if he didn't wish to speak, then he didn't have to.

"I should probably get some work done," she suggested, offering him an out if he wanted it. All he had to do was agree.

"*Nyet.*" He shook his head. "No need until I hear back about the others."

"Then what should we do?" she asked, looking around them and then back to him.

"Listen to the birds," Sergei suggested. "Enjoy the sun on your skin. Smell the air and eat more fruit. This is what I wanted to share with you."

If she hadn't been so curious about his family, Eleanor would have enjoyed the idyllic countryside more. As it was, with so many questions burdening her mind, she found it hard to let go, to truly relax. Just as she prepared to inquire what he was thinking about, he spoke again.

CHAPTER XV

Memories

"Pasha is married," Sergei said. He could tell his words caught Eleanor by surprise, but whether it was what he'd said or the simple fact he'd answered that surprised her was hard to tell. Did she think thieves never married? Well, maybe in the old days the thieves' code forbade marriage, but times had changed. Sergei's own existence was proof enough of how much the culture had shifted over the decades.

"Does his wife know that you're...?" Her question hung on the air.

"Thieves?" He nodded. "Of course."

"And she doesn't have any problem with that?" Eleanor sounded skeptical.

"I wouldn't say she's thrilled about it," he answered. "She loves Pasha, so she's willing to accept certain compromises in order to be with him."

A look of distaste crossed Eleanor's delicate face, like she tasted something foul. She frowned in dismay.

"Something you don't like?" he asked.

"No," she said, but the frown remained firmly planted on her lips, dragging down the corners of her shapely mouth. "I don't know. It's just hard to imagine being with someone who leads a criminal life."

Sergei raised an eyebrow, looking at her and wondering if she'd thought through that statement. "You do realize who you're with, no?"

His question earned a glare from her but it was short-lived. "Obviously," she answered tartly, "I'm not talking about us. We're not married."

"Ah, I see," he cast her a suggestive look as he spoke, reaching out to take hold of her by the hip and pull her closer. "That can be easily remedied, you know. A few calls, a quick registration. You could stay in Russia."

She turned out of his embrace with a forced laugh. "I don't think so," she said, stepping back toward the cherry tree. Diverting her attention from him, she plucked several more of the ripe fruits and popped them in her mouth, stripping the tart flesh and spitting the pits into the overgrown grass.

"Why not?" he asked. "Are you afraid to marry me?"

"Not afraid," Eleanor answered, looking at him and sounding quite serious. "Why? Are you asking me to marry you?"

Catching her wrist, he pulled her back, into his arms where he could hold her. He loved feeling the press of her soft against his chest, inhaling the fragrant scent of her hair as he leaned down to kiss her temple. Nuzzling along her hairline to her ear, he asked her softly, "would you deny me if I did?"

He could feel her heart beating, fast and hard in her chest as she looked up at him. And for a moment, he saw the same regret in her eyes that he'd seen in the hotel room before. It was there and gone in an instant before she shook her head, pressing gently against his chest to step away.

"I used to dream about marrying you," she confessed, tucking her arm around him and standing beside him. His other hand came down to cover hers, stroking gently over her delicate skin as she leaned her head against his shoulder. "Oh yes," she continued when he smirked in amusement. "I had all the details worked out, even had a dress designed in my head. Lord, I don't know what I was thinking, but I loved you so much. I was willing to leave everything in order to follow you to Russia."

"But all that has changed," he predicted.

Eleanor looked at him with sad resignation, then nodded. "I have a life now, a career, and–" she paused, looking uncertain "–and my mom," she finished somewhat lamely.

Sergei regarded her suspiciously. "I don't recall you two being particularly close when I was in the States."

Eleanor shrugged, adopting a look of indifference. "That was seven years ago. I guess I've grown up since then."

He couldn't argue with that. There was no denying that she still responded readily to his advances, but she could stand her ground, too. Still, he wasn't convinced that the tender, passionate girl he loved was entirely gone. There was too much softness in her eyes for her to hide the fact that she remained, at heart, the same. The world had yet to strip the kindness from her, and if he had any input on the matter, it never would.

"Tell me more about your family," she suggested. It seemed a genuine curiosity, even if it served to change the topic away from marriage.

Relenting, he let the subject drop, and asked instead, "what to tell?"

Dima was one of the best safe-breakers in the world, while Pasha could put down half a dozen men by himself, but those weren't the sort of things he was about to tell her. Should he boast of how well Masha could remove a bullet or stitch up a knife wound at home thanks to her years as a nurse? It hardly seemed appropriate. And Anton? Well, there was little enough to say about him. A dissolute drunk with potential he wasted.

"Our father died last year," the words surprised him, coming out before he really thought over what he was saying. "It wasn't unexpected, exactly. But I suppose I was surprised. His health wasn't bad, you know?"

Eleanor cast him a sympathetic look. "I'm sorry, that must have been hard."

"*Da nyet,*" he said, shrugging and tucking his hands into his pockets. "Everyone dies someday. He was seventy-five and went out happy. It's better that way. Olga dying, all the rest of this shit–it would have devastated him.

"*Nu ladno,*" he said, taking a deep breath and exhaling. "Come on, we'll take a walk into the village, I'll show you where babushka taught me to gut fish."

"Sergei, how did you become a criminal?"

After a long afternoon spent walking through the village and the countryside, visiting landmarks from his youth, and an even longer evening spent collecting beans and fruit from the garden before indulging in altogether more carnal delights, they were laying entwined, skin-to-skin in the dark. Eleanor was warm against his side, trailing her fingertips over his skin. The pleasant feeling of her nails just grazing over him put Sergei into a supremely relaxed state. He didn't even hesitate to answer.

"How did you become an American?" he asked.

"I was born there," she answered with a tone like she was stating the obvious.

"There you have it," he said. "I was born into it. With my father, there couldn't be another path in life for me. Call it my destiny, if you will."

His answer didn't seem to satisfy her.

"Tell me about your dad, then," she suggested.

"What do you want to know?" he asked.

"I don't know, anything," she said, turning to rest her chin on his chest. It was impossible for her to see his face as more than a slightly lighter shadow against the darker shadows in the pitch black. There were no ambient street or city lights, and the curtains were firmly drawn to block out any moon or starlight–even he couldn't distinguish anything in such darkness. Still, he could feel her looking up toward his face. "What was he like?"

"Strong. Strict." He paused, trying to let his mind stretch back to childhood for some early recollection. It was hard. So much had happened since then, so many memories that crowded the path between the man he was and the boy he'd once been. "He was protective of the family. Always had to know what everyone was doing, and he loved mom."

"But he was a criminal?" Eleanor sounded like she found it hard to believe.

"It's not the same here," he sighed, stilling her hand to hold it over his heart. "My father was born in a Soviet prison, raised in the midst of common criminals and other scum."

"Your babushka was in prison?" she asked in surprise.

"*Nyet,*" he said. "Lyudmila Alexeievna, the one who owned this house, informally adopted my father when he was in his thirties. His birth parents were sent to the prison camp in the fall of 1939. Dad was born in 1940, just in time for the war. Parents died in the work camps, dad was sent to the children's home for a few years, then back to the gulag for petty crimes. At sixteen, they turned him loose on the streets. The rest, you could say, is history."

"That's awful." Eleanor sounded horrified by his callous summary of events. "I don't understand," she said, "why? What did your grandparents do?"

Sergei turned the bedside lamp on and gave her a rueful look, turning to reveal the bare skin of his back. He could feel her eyes tracing the majestic eagle inked into his skin, and looking over his shoulder at her, he asked, "did you ever wonder why I have this on my body?"

She nodded. "I assumed it was to show your authority."

"*Nu da,*" he agreed. "More importantly, it's the imperial eagle of the Tsar. My father had this tattoo, his father had it, and his grandfather too.

When the bolsheviks started killing everyone, my great-grandfather died fighting for the Whites. The rest of his family, including my grandfather, were sent into exile in the far east. In the '30s he finished his army service, and in 1939 they arrested him and his pregnant wife."

"For what?" Eleanor asked. "That doesn't make any sense."

"Article 58," he said, laying back again and drawing her close against the length of his side. "*Vrag naroda*."

Enemy of the people. The accusation chafed heavily against his blood, but it was clear from her blank expression that Eleanor didn't comprehend the gravity of the term.

"They were deemed enemies of the people," he clarified, "for being in favor of the tsar, once upon a time. For doubting the supreme Soviet power. Thrown into prison to rot to death, and rot they did."

"God Sergei, that's horrible. How old was your father when they died?"

He sat up, shrugging and leaning back against the wall. There was an oriental carpet tacked to the wall where he leaned, just one of many that were tacked to practically every wall in the house. An old-school custom his babushka always practiced to keep the house cool in summer and warm in winter, so he'd maintained it when she died.

"Seven or eight. Saw his father for the last time when he was four, so no one's sure when he died exactly, and his mother died a few years later. He was already in and out of the children's homes by then," he explained. "By the time he was twelve, he'd run away so many times that they caught him and put him back in the prison proper."

"They put a child in prison with adults?" she asked, aghast at the prospect.

"Until he was sixteen," Sergei confirmed. "Then he and Yuriy were tossed out to fend for themselves and warned off ever getting in trouble with the law."

"Yuriy?"

He paused, biting his tongue. It hadn't been his intention to mention Yuriy, but the words slipped out and Eleanor was sharp. She obviously wanted to know more about his life, and anyone in it. Sucking air through his teeth for a moment, he considered how much to tell her.

"My uncle," he said finally. "Yuriy was like my father. Orphaned by the war, sent to a series of children's homes where the kids were starved, crawling with lice, diseased. In some places they slept beside the corpses of the dead for days at a time, before someone would come and clear away the bodies. He had a brother and sister when they went into the home, but they both died. So he ran away, eventually the police caught him too and put him in the gulag. That's how he and my father met during the first year. Together, they found a way to survive."

Eleanor looked like she might be sick. Noticing the nauseous look on her face, Sergei tried to think of something less macabre to discuss. His memories were wide awake though, and it was hard to think of something suitable.

"Suffice to say, not all matters of criminality are so cut and dry," he said. "Especially during the soviet era."

"Indeed not." Eleanor shuddered, turning to sit on the edge of the bed with her feet on the floor. "How could anyone be so cruel to children?"

Sergei didn't answer. He didn't have an answer for her. It was just how things had been during the time before and after the great war. There was no way to understand or justify it. After a moment, Eleanor rose from the bed and went to the kitchen for a glass of water. When she returned, Sergei wrapped her in his arms with a kiss, holding her and stroking up and down along the length of her arm until she fell asleep.

CHAPTER XVI

Departure

In just under twenty-four hours, Eleanor would be boarding a plane at the Moscow Sheremetyevo International Airport to return home. The fact that she'd already used up her limited time in the country felt surreal. It was early evening, and all day Sergei had been sulking around the house due to her refusal to overstay her visa. And she still hadn't told him about Ana.

Speaking–or rather, thinking–of her daughter, she'd only managed to call twice since Sergei took her to the dacha. With his nearly-constant presence, it'd been hard enough to make those two brief calls, but fortunately for Eleanor, her mother had been keeping Ana quite preoccupied. When she got back to the States, she made a mental note to thank her mother with something very nice. Which reminded her...

Aside from a few postcards and a ballerina in a snow globe that she'd picked out in a gift shop near the hotel, Eleanor hadn't done any shopping for gifts. Partly it was because she'd been busy with the case, but she couldn't deny the fact that Sergei had wholly monopolized the rest of her time. It was a fact that had to be remedied before she left the country. After all, she'd promised Ana plenty of presents and she wasn't about to disappoint her little angel.

"Do you know any good shops that we could visit tomorrow?" she asked.

They were in the kitchen, with Eleanor seated in an old wooden chair at the table with an open bottle of wine and their glasses. Sergei was at the counter, preparing ingredients for their dinner–turned out the man was a decent cook, so long as the dish involved some sort of meat. So far they'd eaten lamb, chicken, duck, pork sausages, and beef in a variety of forms. Eleanor was sure the essence of meat would be oozing from her very pores for weeks to come but she didn't mind; everything he'd prepared so far proved to be delicious.

"What do you need?" he asked, scraping a pile of chopped herbs off the cutting board and into a bowl with the side of his knife.

"I'd like to do some gift shopping," she answered honestly. "You know, trinkets and knickknacks, some nice souvenirs."

"Who are we shopping for?" he asked, and she thought she heard an undertone of suspicion in his voice.

"My mother," she said, "and some girlfriends."

"Since when do you have girlfriends?" he asked, cocking an eyebrow at her.

"I don't know, since I live in America and I'm not entirely antisocial?" she asked in return, letting an edge of sarcasm creep into her voice. "When did you join the Spanish Inquisition?"

He laughed at that, nodding agreeably. "*Ladno,* I can take you shopping tomorrow. We'll leave early so you don't miss your flight."

"Thank you," she said, and reached for the bottle of wine to pour generously into her glass. Lifting the over-full glass to her lips, she took a long sip. It was a village wine, as Sergei had informed her, crafted by one of the old men who held on to old methods for fermenting the grapes. She'd never had wine with such a unique flavor–it lingered on her lips and tongue, leaving behind a pleasant, lightly-fruity taste that she couldn't quite identify but nonetheless enjoyed.

She knew Sergei was less than thrilled about her looming departure. It didn't take a behavioral scientist to read his pensive expressions, nor an oracle to divine the reason for his gradually-increasing level of moodiness and malcontent over the previous two days. Summertime in Russia was in full procession but despite the warm weather, he'd spent an hour chopping firewood by the shed that afternoon. As far as venting methods went, Eleanor wasn't going to complain. The fact that he'd looked like a Nordic god whilst doing so was just an added bonus.

Glancing to her laptop, she was reminded of the case that brought her there in the first place. As she'd suspected, all the victims had ties to the criminal world. She had a feeling they were more closely connected than Sergei let on, but she'd decided not to press him too much. Let the man have his secrets. It was his sister who'd been murdered, so if he wanted to avenge the matter he'd have to tell her anything that was important and pertinent to the case.

With the additional information that he had shared with her, Eleanor was able to put all the pieces in place and when Sergei plotted all the murder sites on the map, something clicked. She'd seen the pattern, and realized where the final murder sites would be located. Marking the four remaining sites, she turned the information over to Sergei and Inspector Kossakov. It was hard to tell when the killer would strike, so she'd drawn up a list of the most likely dates for the next year. It made her sick to think it might take so long to catch the one who was responsible, but she hadn't found a precise pattern to the dates of his murders yet so intuitive guesswork was the best she could do. She just hoped she was right.

The sound of meat sizzling as it hit a hot pan drew her attention back to Sergei. Their time together had passed so quickly, Eleanor found it hard to believe. Just as it began to feel like maybe they'd never been apart at all, it was nearly time for her to leave.

Over the course of the week, she'd learned more about Sergei than she could have imagined. It made her heart ache when she realized just how much pain and suffering lingered in his past. Whatever she'd thought before, it didn't come close to the tragic reality of his lineage. The mental image of diseased, emaciated children, simply wasting away in a so-called orphanage, was a hard one to shake from her mind. It was the sort of stuff nightmares were made of, but for his family it had been a reality.

Sergei was right, she decided. There was no way she would have imagined such horrible things. And that was just what he'd been willing to tell her. From the long silences when he talked about his family or past, to the sketchy details about what they did and the source of their wealth, she knew whatever he shared was only the tip of the iceberg.

And as curious as she was, in all honesty Eleanor wasn't sure she wanted to know everything her lover hid. What if he'd done something horrific? As if killing someone isn't horrific enough, she chastised herself. She was relatively certain he'd killed before, yet she'd reconciled herself with that fact and accepted it readily enough. It was reassuring to think he could only have killed scum, but unless she asked there was no way for her to really know.

What she knew was that he was intent on killing whoever murdered his sister. That of course seemed justifiable enough, and even though it had crossed her mind, she'd resolved not to tip anyone off. When in Rome, and all that. But what if he'd killed someone who was innocent? What if he helped sell drugs to teenagers, or got girls involved in prostitution? The illegal trafficking of young girls and prostitutes to and from the former east bloc was one of the more lucrative criminal trades, from what she'd studied. The idea was enough to make her skin crawl.

There was no way. Shaking herself physically in an effort to lose the creeped-out feeling that lingered down the back of her neck, she watched her lover. Sergei couldn't do those sort of things. Not when he was so tender, so passionate and–dare she say–protective toward her. If not for the ink that marked him, who would ever know what lurked behind those crystalline blue eyes? It's impossible.

Sergei was true to his word and they left early the following morning. All the belongings she'd brought with her were neatly packed back into her suitcase, while her ticket and passport were neatly prepared and stored safely in her purse. They left the dacha at just past ten, rolling down the bumpy gravel drive to the paved road beyond, and Eleanor felt a great twinge of regret as they left. She wanted to stay, and more than that, she wanted to share the place with Ana. Every time they'd gone to the country for Halloween pumpkins or u-pick fruit, it'd been nearly impossible to pry her daughter out of the fields. Ana loved animals, running freely, and the clean scent of country air.

"Tell me more about who we're shopping for," Sergei said, stirring her from her thoughts as they cruised along the highway.

Eleanor shifted, glad his eyes were on the road rather than her. Aside from her mother, she only had one close friend to shop for and her supervisor at the criminal psych unit, then it was all Ana.

"Mostly my mom," she answered, trying to sound as nonchalant as possible. "I'd also like to get something nice for Des."

"Who?" he asked.

"Desiree, my best friend," she said.

"Your age?" he inquired.

"Close enough," Eleanor said. "She's a year older than me but we're not counting. We were roommates during college."

Apparently that was enough information to satisfy him. They lapsed into a comfortable silence as the wild countryside fell away behind them. First it gave way to cultivated fields, giving way to numerous villages and towns as they drove until they were back on the streets of Moscow. A veteran of the busy roads, Sergei soon pulled onto a quiet side street and parked close to the curb. Eleanor looked around for some sign of the expected tourist shops, but only saw what looked like typical Russian storefronts with their weathered signs in faded Cyrillic script. Sergei came around and opened her door, holding out his hand to her.

"This way," he said, pulling her to his side. The door clicked shut behind her, locking automatically, and Sergei escorted her down the street to a discreet, unassuming storefront. The front window was foggy with dust and the usual city grime, partially obscuring a case of lacquered cigar boxes and silver cigarette cases with fine, intricate engravings. When they entered the store, a bell chimed to announce their arrival, and Sergei greeted a short, middle-aged woman in Russian.

"Welcome to the Golden Rose Boutique. Go on, take a look around while I have a talk with Sarnai," he encouraged her, indicating the stout, Asian-faced lady sitting on her stool behind the main counter. The woman, Sarnai, looked happy to see Sergei and greeted him with familiar warmth even as she cast a curious, interested eye on Eleanor.

Talk about not judging a book by its cover... If Sergei hadn't taken her to the unassuming shop, Eleanor knew she never would have found a place like the Golden Rose. It's outward appearance was deceptive, to say the least. Inside, the store was impeccably clean and absolutely packed with a wide variety of merchandise, most of which Eleanor had never seen the likes of before. Rather than feeling crowded by the way space in the shop had been used to the maximum, Eleanor found the atmosphere cozy and private. Of course, the fact that they were the only patrons at present amplified that feeling.

Near the back of the shop were several racks of clothing, a wide variety of finery for children hung off the back wall on display hangers. Eleanor gravitated toward the clothes, stunned by the finery of the fabrics and the detailed stitching. It was clear that whoever made such garments put an enormous amount of time and care into them. Looking at a particularly lovely dress that she knew would fit her best friend perfectly, she hesitated to look at the price tag, then took the plunge and flipped it over.

A multi-thousand total was the first thing she laid eyes on and she was about to set the dress back on its rack when she realized the price was in roubles. Below the local currency, the prices in euros and dollars were listed. $225.– the tag read. It was an eye-watering amount to pay for a dress, but she'd known going to Moscow that it was an expensive city, and allocated up to $300 to get Desiree something nice. Tucking the dress gently over her arm, she decided to hold onto it unless something better caught her eye and continued on to browse the children's clothes.

The wall of tiny suits and dresses for little boys and girls looked like something out of a royal wardrobe, and on a table in front of the wall there were various tiny shoes lined up and waiting to be matched with one of the outfits hanging above. Reaching up, Eleanor lifted a white dress with pearls stitched into the fabric and a mix of golden and silver thread from its place on the wall, bringing it down to look at it more closely. It was Ana's size, perhaps a touch big but that wouldn't hurt with how fast the girl grew. The dress was short-sleeved, lined with a soft taffeta lace, and zipped up the back with silken ribbons at the waist tied into a bow at the back. Flipping the price tag over, she stifled a snort. $350.–

Of course it's more expensive than the dress with three times as much fabric. She wasn't surprised. Over the years, she'd grown accustomed to paying as much for Ana's clothes as she paid for her own, oftentimes more. For some reason, manufacturers seemed to think it was perfectly acceptable to mark up kids' clothes to obscene levels. Probably because fools like me will still pay. She sighed, stretching to return the dress to its spot on the wall. It was gorgeous, to be sure, but she didn't want to spend half her budget for Ana on one present.

Circling around the shop some more to look at what else was available, Eleanor admired a selection of bronze broaches, each of them crafted into a unique, knotted design. There were golden hair pins that looked like they came from Asia or the east of the country, and a selection of Mongolian mouth harps alongside an array of wooden smoking pipes, each a delicately-carved beauty. In a case near the main desk, where Sergei and the shopkeeper sat talking, several trays of rings, earrings, and dazzling jeweled necklaces sat beside silver keepsake boxes lined in velvet.

At a loss, Eleanor returned to the clothes near the back, passing a case of polished goblets and crystal wine glasses on the way. In another case there were hand-painted porcelain tea sets, each cup with a matching lid and saucer to go with it. Oh, if only she had unlimited funds!

Sergei found her deliberating over clothes at the back of the store. Aside from the dress she was certainly going to purchase for Desiree, and the wondrous white creation that she could already see on Ana, a coat rack with several coats and lined capes had caught her eye.

"I see you've found something to your liking," Sergei observed, looking over the items she'd picked out. "Children's clothes?" he asked with a raised brow.

"Erm, yeah," she said, scrambling for an excuse. "It's, ah, Des' daughter. I promised to bring her back something special."

Glancing over the items she'd picked out, he nodded but still seemed skeptical. "Are you close?"

"Huh?" Eleanor looked at him in confusion.

"To your friend's daughter," he prompted, gesturing to the dress she'd picked out and the silk-lined black cape she was agonizing over. It was the most affordable item from the coat rack at just $150, but she didn't usually dress Ana in black.

"Very close," she confirmed, trying not to sound too attached at the same time. "I've known her ever since she was a baby." That much was true.

"Then if I may," he said, picking up the cloak. "You want something to go with the dress?"

Eleanor nodded and Sergei turned back to the rack, replacing the cloak and looking through the other items for something of a similar size. After a minute, he turned back to her with a stunning two-tone cloak, red on the outside and fully lined with the softest, cream-colored fur on the inside.

"This matches the dress much better, wouldn't you agree?" he asked, presenting the cloak to her. "It also has a hood and pockets for the girl."

Eleanor sighed, looking from the cloak to the dress and back again. She knew there was no way she'd be able to afford both, and it was hard to tell which one Ana would want more. Reaching out, she felt the soft outer fabric, then stroked gently over the fur lining, before reaching for the price tag.

"*Ne nado,*" Sergei said, pulling it out of her reach before she could flip the tag over. "Just say you like it, the price doesn't matter."

Eleanor blanched, staring at him in shock. "You can't be serious. Please, I budgeted for presents." She reached again but he held the red cloak out of her reach, calling something to Sarnai in Russian.

"Indulge me, Nora," he said, catching her hand and raising it to his lips to kiss the back gently. "I have to let you go in just a few hours, let me do this much."

"Sergei—"

"*Tikho, tikho,*" he silenced her softly, reaching for the dress she'd picked out and taking that too. "Don't argue this time."

She sighed, shaking her head first before nodding in agreement.

"As you wish, my lord," she acquiesced.

"Mm, now why couldn't you be so agreeable when I asked you to stay?" he asked, his tone somewhere between serious and teasing.

Resting her hand on the front of his chest, she leaned up and kissed him gently on the cheek. "Because I'm not ready to give up my whole life just yet." Which was mostly true. "Maybe you should come back to the US..."

"Are you inviting me?" he asked.

"If you need an invitation, then yes," she said.

Silence reigned between them for a long moment, his gaze fixed steadily on her. "Then maybe I will," he informed her with a suggestive smirk, then gestured to the table behind her. "Anything else? Does the girl need shoes to go with her new outfit?"

"Oh no," Eleanor said assuredly. Not only was she not keen to spend Sergei's money, Ana had plenty of shoes. Indeed, her delicate little feet seemed to be the only thing that didn't grow like a weed. For years, Ana topped the growth charts at the 102nd percentile for her age group, and growing taller with every day.

At Sergei's insistence, they spent another hour browsing through the shop and selecting additional presents for Desiree, Ana, and her mother. With each selection that Sergei swiped away to have the shopkeeper tally and pack, Eleanor felt her sense of guilt grow, but it was impossible to deny him. She tried not to think about how he might react if he ever found out the truth.

"Sergei, please," she insisted. "I won't have enough room in my carry-on for everything, and who knows what customs will think." They were up to two dresses for Desiree, five for Ana, a jeweled necklace with matching bracelet and embroidered silk shawl for her mother, and three dresses that he'd picked out for her. Half the items he'd snatched away so quickly that she didn't catch a glimpse of their price tags, but she was certain the amount would give her heart palpitations.

"*Khorosho, davai,*" he said agreeably, draping an arm loosely over her shoulders to guide them back to Sarnai at the checkout. All the items were neatly packed and after a brief exchange in Russian, the dark-haired woman smiled broadly, revealing a row of shining gold teeth, and wished them a fond farewell. Eleanor never saw the bill.

CHAPTER XVII

Stateside

A heavy feeling sat in her gut as Eleanor settled into her assigned seat on the flight that would take her home. She had a two-hour layover in France, then it was a straight line home to the US. It was hard to wrap her mind around the fact that she would be back on the other side of the world within sixteen hours. Reaching down to her right hand, she felt the foreign object on her ring finger, twirling the smooth band around and around. Raising her hand to feel her lips, she closed her eyes, savoring the lingering sensations of her lover's final kiss.

Sergei had seen her through the first security check when they arrived at the airport, but couldn't proceed any further. Pulling her aside before the second check, he'd pressed her back against a wall of marble, kissing her so passionately she wondered if he was trying to take part of her soul in the process. And then he'd knelt before her, withdrawing a small, black box.

"Wait before you protest," he said, presenting the open box. It contained an engagement ring, a band of white gold that wrapped elegantly around three small stones with a single, medium-sized diamond set in the center. Catching the light of the wide, open atrium, each exquisitely-cut gemstone glittered as he tilted the box.

"Say you'll marry me," he said, reaching for her right hand as he held her gaze. He hadn't risen from his knee, and he continued before she could protest, "I'm not saying right here or right now. Just agree that you will."

Conflicting feelings waged a battle for dominance over her heart, excitement that ached with pain. Say no! But she couldn't bring herself to do it.

"Sergei," she breathed. What would she tell her mother, or Ana? Or him, for that matter. "How can I possibly say yes?"

"Because I'll come for you, one way or another. When I'm done here, and I've settled all my debts." The intensity in his eyes underlined his statement, spoken just loud enough for her alone to hear. "Say yes, Nora."

"I can't," she whispered, feeling tortured as the words left her lips. Trying to pull her hand away, she was surprised by the sudden strength in Sergei's grip as he held her wrist. His hold wasn't quite painful, but it was tight, unrelenting, and her gaze jumped to his in surprise.

"You can," he stated, rising from his knee to tower over her. "And you will. You're already mine. *Slyshish menya?*" Taking the ring from its box with his other hand, he slid the cool metal over the ring finger of her right hand. "I don't care what you're hiding in America; I will come for you."

What was she going to tell her mother? Eleanor still hadn't decided whether to take the ring off by the time her plane was circling to land in Seattle. On the one hand, it didn't look too obscenely expensive; she could conceivably pass it off as a personal souvenir that she just couldn't live without. On the other hand, it really did look like the engagement ring it was. Then again, it's on my right hand... and her mother didn't know the first thing about Russian orthodox beliefs or the difference in ring placement.

The ring stayed on right up until she was ready to disembark, whereupon Eleanor promptly chickened out. There was no way her mother would buy her flimsy excuse, and then the torrent of questions and semi-informed speculation would never end. Hiding the ring in an inner pocket of her purse, she waited for the other passengers to thin out ahead of her before joining the flow to exit the plane. Processing through customs went blessedly smoothly, a fact for which she was immeasurably thankful. After Sergei left her to proceed through security and customs in Russia, Eleanor had enjoyed the heart-attack inducing experience of declaring all the gifts and last-minute purchases she had in her carry-on bag. Uncertain how much each item had cost, she'd estimated the totals and held her breath, hoping that the customs officials would accept her declaration. In the end, she needn't have worried. The American authorities checked the documents to verify the origin of the furs that'd been used to make Ana's cape, then sent her on her way.

Cleared by customs, she departed to the baggage claim to find her suitcase. No sooner had she approached the carousel then an excited shriek issued across the baggage claim and a small, blond-haired blur raced toward her.

"Mama!" Ana flung herself at Eleanor, who barely had time to drop her purse and carry-on in time to sweep her daughter into a bear hug. "Welcome home, I'm so glad you're finally back!"

Squeezing her tight, Eleanor showered her daughter's cheeks and forehead with kisses. "So am I, baby bear. Thanks for coming to meet me," she said to her own mother as she set Ana down. "I hear the whale watching went well."

"We saw an orca pod, and two humpback whales, a mom and baby," Ana said excitedly, seizing hold of her right hand as Eleanor picked up her purse and carry-on with the other.

"Welcome home, darling. Do you have any other bags?" her mother asked. "We already got this one." She indicated Eleanor's large, red suitcase that contained the rest of her belongings and two of the dresses she hadn't been able to fit in the carry-on.

"Yep, that's everything," Eleanor confirmed with a smile. "Thanks Mom. Here, let's trade, this one's lighter."

Handing off the duffel bag she used as a carry-on to her mother, she took her suitcase and gestured for her mother to lead the way while Ana carried her purse, proudly slung over her tiny shoulder.

It was half-past ten when they finally got home that night. After four years of living in a one-room apartment in the city center, Eleanor had moved with her daughter to a duplex in the suburbs two years ago. It was one of the best decisions she'd ever made, allowing Ana to have a back yard (even if it was the size of a postage stamp) and her own room, not that it stopped her from crawling into Eleanor's bed any time she couldn't sleep. At least it gave her somewhere to put all the toys that'd previously been scattered everywhere.

Helping her inside with her luggage and a very sleepy Ana, who had dozed off during the drive home, Eleanor's mother embraced her warmly. "Give me a call when you're up in the morning, so I don't worry," she said, kissing her atop the head.

"I will," Eleanor assured her. "Are you sure you don't want your presents now?"

"Not tonight dear, I'll wait," her mother assured her with a smile. "Now go take care of Ana, before the poor girl falls asleep standing."

"Alright." She pulled her mother into another hug, squeezing the older woman gently. "Thank you, Mom. For everything."

Exchanging kisses on the cheek, they parted and Eleanor stood in the door to watch her mother leave. Once her car pulled around the corner and out of sight, she closed the door, locking it and turning to find Ana curled up on the couch. She'd kicked off her shoes but still wore the light jacket her grandma dressed her in, with her own little suitcase abandoned by the front door.

"Can I have my presents?" she asked, looking up with tired, shining eyes.

Eleanor laughed, stepping out of her own shoes to come and kneel by her daughter. "Hm, Grandma says you were good the whole time I was gone, but I have my doubts."

Ana sat up, excitement fueling a fresh burst of energy. "I was good!"

"Are you sure?" Eleanor teased, tickling her sides lightly. "Because I think she wouldn't tell me if you were a naughty gremlin, would she? After all, you're her very favorite granddaughter."

"She would," Ana insisted solemnly. "I'm her only granddaughter, but Grandma never lies."

"Hm," she pretended to deliberate for a moment longer, then declared, "alright, I'll be back. You stay here, okay?"

"Okay," Ana agreed, nodding affirmatively.

Heaving her luggage the rest of the way to her room, she set the duffel bag on her bed and unzipped it, pulling out the dresses for Ana. In addition to the white dress she'd picked out first, Sergei had insisted on four more dresses in turquoise, ruby red, emerald green, and golden bronze embroidered with a pattern of leaves. They were stunning dresses, even if she cringed to think of how much they must have cost. Hiding the other dresses at the back of her closet, she unpacked the cloak and laid it beside the white dress. If she hadn't known better, Eleanor would've said the dress and cloak were made for each other. Sergei had an exceptional eye.

Deciding that the other presents could wait, along with unpacking of the rest of her luggage, she pulled a neatly stored gift bag from the top shelf in the closet. Folding up the dress and cloak into as small and neat a bundle as she could manage, she wrestled them into the gift bag and went back out to Ana.

Apparently five minutes of waiting was five minutes too long for Ana, though. When she stepped out, Eleanor found her daughter curled on her side, snuggling a throw pillow and sound asleep. Setting the bag down, she crouched beside Ana and stroked her hair softly. The child didn't stir, so Eleanor eased her out of her jacket and carried her to bed. Changing her into a pair of soft pajamas, she folded back the blankets and tucked her in. Then, stepping softly to avoid making any noise, she retrieved the gift bag from the living room and put it by Ana's bed for her to find in the morning.

Sitting gingerly at the foot of the bed, she watched her daughter sleep, illuminated by the low light from the hall. Exhaustion and jet lag were setting in, but Sergei's words haunted her. How could he know she was hiding something from him? Eleanor was sure she hadn't been so transparent. Probably thinks I have a boyfriend, she sighed, rubbing her eyes. Having a boyfriend would have made the situation a million times simpler. She could dump a boyfriend. How was she supposed to explain Ana?

Casting her daughter a final glance, she rose and crossed the hall to her room, turning the light off as she went. Every muscle in her body seemed to ache, the powerful lure of sleep beckoning her to bed, but she had to wash off the grime and filth of international travel before she could sleep so she tied her hair up and trudged toward the shower. She soaped and scrubbed every inch of her skin, struggling not to fall asleep under the soothing stream of hot water in the process, and emerged clean ten minutes later. It might as well have been ten hours. Clean pajamas were on and her bed was waiting. There was only one thing left to do.

Stealing out to the living room, she retrieved her purse, unzipping it to retrieve the ring he'd given her. It glittered in the light when she pulled it out, and she felt her heart skip a beat as tears welled in her eyes.

She knew it was the exhaustion, knew she needed to just go to bed and sleep because everything was better–or at least, easier to deal with–in the morning, with a good cup of coffee, but she couldn't stop the feeling of abject loss that welled forth from the center of her chest. For seven years she'd convinced herself that everything was fine, that she didn't need him. She made Ana her life, and she was happy. Mostly.

Now he was gone again. This time with promises, but who knew if–or when–those promises would be kept. Would his resolve remain once they'd been apart a few days, weeks? What if it took months, or longer? He'd left her once, and they only met again by chance. What if he vanished forever this time?

Enough, she scolded herself for allowing such a train of thought. Closing her hand around the ring, she left her purse on the couch, turned off the last of the lights, and gave in to the need for sleep.

CHAPTER XVIII

Vengeance

FIVE MONTHS LATER

Silence reigned between the Ivanov brothers as they drove quietly through the night. The clock read 3:17AM. It was over. Pasha was at the wheel, Dima in the passenger seat and Sergei seated behind him in the middle row. Beside him, the body of an unconscious girl lay slumped across the seat. Whatever she'd been drugged with was strong enough to keep her out for hours, more than enough time for her killer to complete his work. From the look of it, she was young, in her mid-twenties perhaps. She would have been the tenth, except that this time they'd been waiting.

Nyet, he corrected himself. Not the tenth. Perhaps the tenth in this horrific ritual his diseased 'cousin' had been carrying out, but he knew for a fact that Gleb's body count was far higher. Glancing over his shoulder, he stared at the unmoving body sprawled uncomfortably across the back. He'd never forget the look of surprise on the bastard's face when they caught him.

"Do you think he's still alive?" Dima asked quietly. If he was concerned, it was only because they wouldn't be able to torture a corpse. They'd bound and gagged Gleb so tightly that he could barely breathe, never-mind trying to shout or protest. If he suffocated before they arrived at their destination, it would be a blessing he didn't deserve.

"He lives," Sergei answered with certainty. He hadn't realized Yuriy's nephew was capable of such filth before, but he'd known other men cast from the same mold. They were like cockroaches. You could beat them, burn them or spoon-feed them poison and still they lived.

"Not for long," Pasha commented softly. "Where do we leave the girl?"

"There's a hospital in the town ahead, pull off and we'll drop her in the ER," Sergei said. The detour only took a matter of minutes, just long enough for Dima to slip into the ER and pass off the unconscious girl. She'd wake up alone in a foreign town, but she had her life and the nurses would make sure she got back in contact with her family. That was more than could be said for the rest of Gleb's victims.

"He's alive," Pasha confirmed, tugging the hood from Gleb's head but leaving the gag firmly in place. Ruby-faced with rage, the immobilized man glared hatefully at the brothers as they made themselves comfortable around him.

They'd made it to their destination, a safe house in a small village not far from the family dacha. They were in a cellar, with Gleb hog-tied and face down on the moist ground as they prepared the area around him. Sergei disliked using the location for such an unsavory task, but they didn't feel like wasting time with the long drive to a more suitable location.

"Here are the sheets," Dima said, entering the cellar with a roll of heavy-gauge plastic sheeting in one hand and scissors in the other. Sergei nodded, and together they stretched out several layers across the floor, pausing only once to move Gleb out of their way. His attempts to thrash out, loosen his bindings, or chew through the gag in order to spit obscenities at them were in vain, and Sergei saw the mounting panic in his eyes as they continued, heard the fear in his labored breathing.

"Olga treated you like a brother," Sergei said, standing over the captive murderer. "Always told us to include you, to treat you like part of the family, because you were so poor and so sad, because you had nothing. Do I remember correctly?"

Gleb stared at him with the wild, glazed eyes of someone gone half-mad. Of course, he'd have to be to have done what he did. Snot clogged his breathing, making the wretch choke.

"I should torture you," Sergei continued, using the sole of his boot to shove Gleb onto his side as he knelt over him, bringing his knee to within an inch of his face. "I should do to you what you did to her, and all the rest of them. Cut your tongue out, sew your mouth shut, and let you suffocate on your own blood before I drain you like a pig. You deserve it, don't you, Gleb?"

Dima and Pasha waited. As much as they loved and cared for Olga (and they did, beyond words) it was clear that this one was in Sergei's hands and his adoptive brothers were ready to assist as needed, but hesitant to interfere otherwise. As they watched, Sergei reached down and loosened the gag, freeing Gleb's ability to breathe and speak.

"Fuck you," he swore, spitting at Sergei from his prone position. "You don't have the stomach, and your sister was a whore."

His words earned Gleb a smashing blow from Sergei's knee. It was swift and hard, with just enough force to smash his nose and fracture several bones without causing fatal brain damage in the process. The resulting bellow of agony and curses was silenced by the thick, earthen walls of the cellar. Sergei gripped Gleb's head by the hair, lifting his face as it streamed with blood and mucus, forcing him to meet his eyes.

"This is your only chance," he said. There was no remorse in his voice or his eyes, it was just a simple fact. "Beg me for a swift death."

"*Poshel ty–*" Gleb spat through the blood and pain.

Sergei dropped his face back onto the ground, eliciting more swears. Blood was beginning to pool on the plastic already, spurts of it staining his pants and shirt front. With a feeling of heavy resignation, he turned to Dima.

"Bring me his toolkit."

Valentina Marlova, formerly Sverlova, was not the sort of woman who generally accepted unscheduled guests. In fact, she rather made a point of turning away anyone who was so rude as to show up at her home uninvited. So it came as no surprise to Sergei when she initially refused to admit him.

"Oh Valya," Sergei singsonged through the intercom as he stood at her front door. The woman had done quite well for herself. After enrolling in the Moscow State Technical Institute specifically with the goal of landing a decent man, she'd walked down the aisle on the arm of a resident surgeon already making his way up the promotions ladder and never looked back. Their miniature mansion on the outskirts of the city was just private enough to afford the illusion of being in the countryside.

"Get lost before I call the police," her voice came back full of venom.

"You know I'm immune to your threats, now open up unless you want a real scandal," he ordered, shifting the gift bag he held from one hand to the other.

There was silence, but within minutes he heard the clicking of her shoes as she approached and then the lock being slid aside. A moment later the door swung open, revealing Valentina in all her glory. With her auburn hair twisted stylishly atop her head and wearing two-and-a-half inch heels, she almost rivaled Sergei in height.

"What the hell do you want?" she demanded, standing firm in the doorway. Her critical gaze swept over him, waiting for an answer.

"Invite me inside for tea," he suggested, handing her the gift bag. "I brought you a present."

A look of surprise flashed across her face before she could conceal it. Still eyeing him with suspicion, she accepted the gift bag. She didn't rush to open it, but did step aside to let Sergei enter. He didn't plan on staying long, so he left his shoes on and followed Valentina to the kitchen.

"I must admit you caught me by surprise," she said, setting the gift bag down on the counter and turning to set water to boil. "What's the occasion?" Her tone was civil but it was a false civility. Sergei knew she couldn't stand his presence in her home, and that every moment he lingered was one too many.

"Tell me where your father is hiding and I'll be out of your hair," he answered, catching her look of satisfaction at his words. "Clearly you already suspected my motive, if that look is anything to go by. And you know where he is."

"Even if I did, you should know better than to think I'll tell you," Valentina answered. Her tone was saccharine, full of fake sweetness and derision. "Oh come now, Sergei. You of all people should know that I will never be a turncoat on my father like our dear little Lila. Normal people, you see, actually love their family and want what's best for them."

"We'll see about that," Sergei said softly, nodding toward the gift bag. "Why don't you take a look at your present."

Valentina sniffed, rolling her eyes theatrically as she approached the bag. "There is nothing in the world you could ever bribe me with, Sergei. Look around, I have everything I could possibly want!"

"Yes, I'm sure." Sergei nodded, gesturing for her to get on with it already. Casting him a look of pure disdain, she proceeded to unpack the gift bag, pulling out balls of tissue paper first before reaching in to lift out the plastic-wrapped object in the bag. For a moment she looked confused, then sheer panic and revulsion filled her face.

"Are you out of your fucking mind?!" she screamed, dropping the plastic-wrapped head of her cousin in disgust. Gleb's lifeless eyes stared through the thick plastic, looking into nothing as Valentina continued screaming.

"Be quiet," Sergei snapped, catching hold of her and forcing her onto a stool at the counter. Turning off the water boiler, he picked up the severed head and dropped it back into the bag, covering it over with tissue paper again, and then turned his attention back to Valentina. "Now let's try this conversation again. Where is Yuriy?"

"What, so you can do that to him too?" she asked, gesturing toward the gift bag with her chin and a shudder. The blood had drained from her face, leaving her already-pale skin an inhuman shade of white. "What the fuck is wrong with you?"

"Your cousin is the one who murdered Olga," Sergei spat, seizing her by the shoulders to shake her. "Now tell me where to find your father or you're going to join them!"

It wasn't true. Sergei only had to take one look in Valentina's terrified eyes to be reminded that he could never hurt her, no matter how much of a raging bitch she'd turned into over the years. But her terror was real, and in the next moment she began blubbering hopelessly.

"He's in St. Petersburg," she confessed. Taking a pen and paper from a nearby drawer, she scribbled the address down for him, holding it out with a shaking hand.

"Thank you," he said, taking it from her. "Was that so hard?" Pulling his phone out, he called Pasha to come in from the car.

"He's in St. Petersburg," Sergei informed his brother when he entered the kitchen. "Keep an eye on her until we get there."

Valentina looked ready to panic again. "Wait, Pasha can't stay here. What am I supposed to tell my husband?"

Sergei glanced at his watch. "It's only a six-hour drive. Behave yourself and Pasha will leave as soon as we arrive. Unless of course you'd like to come with us," he suggested.

"You'll all go to prison someday," she replied, folding her arms across her chest in defiance and glaring darkly at him.

"I'll call you when we get there," he said to Pasha, ignoring her commentary. Picking up the gift bag with Gleb's head, he turned back to Valentina. "Thank you for your assistance." And on a more serious, somber note he added, "I'm not going to hurt Yuriy, so don't give Pasha any trouble."

Dima was waiting in the drive, having taken Pasha's place behind the wheel. He looked to Sergei for direction as he took the passenger seat, placing their gift bag on the back seat. "Where to?"

Sergei met his brother's gaze with a look of grim determination. "St. Petersburg. He's at the old Primorsky manor."

CHAPTER XIX

Yuriy

"Think he'll finally hear us out?" Dima asked.

They'd reached the old manor where, according to Valentina, their adoptive uncle was hiding out. Sergei couldn't help but admire the man's brazen choice for his getaway. The manor was located in St. Peterburg's Primorsky district, not exactly a low-profile location but it'd worked out for Yuriy. While they were busy checking high and low for Yuriy in all the safe houses and countryside hides, they hadn't bothered to check the old manor in the city.

"He'll listen," Sergei said, reaching for the red gift bag in the seat behind him. Picking up his phone, he dialed Pasha to confirm their arrival, then turned to Dima once he'd hung up. "Shall we?"

Stepping out of the car, he waited for his brother to join him and together they strode up the stone walkway to the grand double doors that provided entry to the splendid, palatial home. An ornate, brass door-knocker hung on the right hand door, and Sergei didn't hesitate to use it.

"The door is open," a familiar voice answered from the intercom set into the wall beside the door. Exchanging a look with Dima, he shrugged. Either Yuriy was prescient, or Valentina must have tipped her father off.

Entering the grand foyer, they spotted Yuriy standing at the top of the sweeping staircase with a half-full glass of vodka in hand. He was dressed casually, in soft house slippers and a robe worn over matching silk pajamas. Judging by the silver beard adorning his face, it'd been a few weeks since his last encounter with a razor.

"Come up," Yuriy beckoned them with his free hand. "It's about time."

Dima looked at Sergei as if to ask 'what the hell?' but Sergei was equally at a loss. If he'd been waiting for them, why would Yuriy have left in the first place? It wasn't like the man had gone on a sabbatical. He'd pulled a straight-up vanishing act, and taken more than two hundred documents with him. Important documents. Incriminating documents.

When they reached the top of the stairs, Yuriy was already halfway down the hall, leading the way to the study. It was more of a library, in actual fact, what with the book collection Yuriy had amassed over the preceding twenty years, but it still served as his study when the manor was occupied. It hadn't changed from the last time Sergei was there, some three years prior, with the possible exception of a growing layer of dust atop the bookcases. In the center of the great room was still Yuriy's desk, a mammoth that'd been hand-carved, crafted out of a single black walnut tree, with several leather wingback chairs arranged at intervals around it.

Several books were open on the table, beside them a stack with several more, and two more glasses waited next to an open bottle of vodka. Yuriy poured for them, handed them each a glass, and finally spoke, "I propose a toast, if I may. To the family."

"What's to say you didn't poison the bottle?" Dima asked suspiciously, regarding Yuriy with distrust.

The elder man didn't bother to answer. Picking up the bottle, he brought it directly to his lips and took three large drinks before setting it back on the table with a bang. Turning his attention back to Sergei, he held up his glass again, wiping the back of his hand across his mouth. "As I said: to the family."

Nodding, Sergei clinked his glass, nudging Dima to loosen up and do the same. In unison, the three men downed their shots. As he poured another round into their glasses, Yuriy continued, "what's in the bag?"

Sergei had almost forgotten the weight of Gleb's head in the gift bag he carried. Setting it on the table, he lifted his glass. "If I may," he said. "To Olga, may she rest in peace now that vengeance is done."

His toast must have surprised Yuriy. The old man raised one heavy brow at him, but only hesitated for a moment before downing the shot. Setting aside his glass and the bottle, he reached for the bag and pulled it closer.

"You've dealt with the killer, then?" he asked, testing the weight of the bag. Sergei nodded, setting aside his own glass as he watched, waiting for Yuriy's reaction. It only took a moment for his uncle to remove the tissue paper and peer inside the bag. He didn't recoil like Valentina had when he realized what the bag contained. Grimacing, he leaned down instead, trying to get a clear view of the face through the plastic.

"Gleb," he sighed heavily in recognition, pushing the bag away. Sergei felt a twinge of regret for approaching Yuriy in such a fashion. The elderly man before him seemed to be a phantom of his former self, aged beyond recognition. He looked tired, with a heavily lined face only half-hidden by his beard. His once light-brown hair matched the silver of his beard, and he turned his weary blue eyes to Sergei as he asked, "how did this happen?"

"In a cellar, with a hatchet," Dima offered helpfully, reaching for the vodka to pour himself another shot. Taking the bottle and his glass, he turned and took up the nearest seat. Sergei replaced the tissue paper and set the bag beneath the table, out of direct sight.

"He was the one murdering people and putting on a freak show with their bodies," Sergei informed Yuriy.

Looking drained of energy, Yuriy moved to take a seat himself, easing into the chair a few feet from Dima. Leaning back, he closed his eyes and folded his hands in front of his belly, slightly rounded now with age and the relaxation of his once-strict physical regimen. "Yes, he always did have an interest in those occult superstitions," he said after a moment of silence.

"Did you know?" Sergei asked. He was the only one left standing as he leaned back against the table, gaze fixed steadily on his uncle.

Yuriy opened his eyes to look at him. "I nursed your sister in my arms when your mother was too sick to care for her. Do you think I wouldn't have cut him into pieces myself if I'd known?"

"Then why have you been holed up here hiding like a rat?" Dima demanded.

"Dima," Sergei said, his tone a warning for his brother to back off. "We've drunk to family. We are family. Let us act like family."

"Speak for yourself, Seryozha," Dima muttered.

"Knock it off," he said, returning his attention to Yuriy. "But he does have a point, Uncle. Where are the files you took?"

He was being diplomatic. If he accused Yuriy of outright theft, it would only serve to insult and put him on the defensive.

"In a safe place," Yuriy assured him. "Have you reconsidered your decision about Lila?"

"No," Sergei stated flatly. "Nor will I."

Yuriy let out a heavy breath, obviously disappointed. "It was your father's dying wish."

"And I told him the same thing I tell you: no. It's been so many years—why do you still press on this?" he asked.

"Because," Yuriy said, "you have never given a substantial reason for your refusal."

Dima snorted but didn't add any further commentary. This was Sergei's battle to wage.

"I don't love her," Sergei stated firmly.

"Yes you do."

"Not as a wife, Yuriy," Sergei said, feeling his frustration mount. His uncle made him feel like he was sixteen years old again, a kid being told what to do and getting reprimanded for being too young or too stupid to see what was ostensibly right in front of him. It didn't sit well. "Now tell me why you took the documents."

"You know why I took them," Yuriy scoffed.

"As insurance?" Sergei regarded him skeptically as Yuriy nodded. "For what?"

"The future," he answered cryptically. "What do you think, Seryozh?" He let his words hang in the air for a minute before continuing. "Marry Lila and I'll return everything. Consider it a wedding present."

His fist clenched, eager to strike someone or something. In an effort to vent his mounting aggression, he turned to pound the table soundly. Once, twice, after a third blow he turned his attention back to Yuriy.

"Why can't you let it go?" he demanded angrily. "What right do you have to make dictates about my life, Yura? Who made you a god?"

"You have!" Yuriy declared vehemently. "The situation might be different if you at least expressed interest in someone else, if you'd taken another woman as wife. But what else do you expect when every year passes and it's still the same?"

"If I had another woman," Sergei echoed. He exhaled, shaking his head and reaching up to run his hands through his hair in agitation. "Alright, if I had another woman," he repeated. "A wife. All this would be settled, yes?"

"You don't have another woman," Yuriy scoffed. "Believe me, Vasya and I checked."

"I said, all of this would be settled, yes?" he demanded sharply, ignoring the comment about his father. "You would return the missing documents?"

Yuriy regarded him speculatively for a moment, then nodded slowly. "Theoretically speaking, yes."

"And if I tell you to hand them over or join your nephew in that bag?" he asked.

He knew the answer just by looking at his uncle. Yuriy crossed one knee over the other, shaking his head just once.

"Killing me would be a grave mistake, but you already know that," he said calmly. Rising from his seat, he continued amicably, "I'll see you out now. Think it over, but don't take too long; my health isn't what it used to be."

"Why don't you just marry the poor girl?" Masha half-asked, half-suggested as they discussed their meeting with Yuriy. They'd made it home late that night, having swung through the city to pick up Pasha on the way back. "I mean, if she's still willing of course."

"This topic is not open for discussion," Sergei informed her shortly.

"Then what is?" she asked tartly. Masha didn't like being shut up. "Because from the sound of it, if he dies before you two come to terms, those papers are going to come back to haunt you. Personally, I wouldn't gamble about it. Marry her, get the documents back, and then file for divorce."

"You assume Yuriy would simply hand everything over," Sergei said. "Do you really think he's so stupid? No. Marrying Lila is off the table, get it out of your head."

"Well then you better start looking for a wife," Masha said seriously. "Because I don't see a way out of this for you. Not unless you really intend to start a war with him."

"He's old, Mash. Like, ancient," Dima piped up, sounding totally unconcerned. "What sort of fight could he possibly put up?"

"Don't underestimate him," Pasha warned. "Look how much leverage he already has over us."

"We're not going to fight with him," Sergei said. His tone was one of finality.

"You have a better idea?" Dima asked.

"I'll give him what he wants," he answered simply, rising from the stool he'd been sitting on. Fetching a bottle of vodka and four glasses from the cupboard, he poured a generous shot into each glass and handed them to his brothers and sister-in-law. "To marriage."

Pasha and Masha drank with him, while Dima hesitated. "To Lila?" he looked as incredulous as he sounded and Sergei couldn't help but laugh loudly.

"Never," he stated, pouring himself another shot.

Dima downed the shot before asking, "then who?"

Masha was waiting too, eager to hear what he would say. Only Pasha looked at him in quiet contemplation, and Sergei had a strange feeling that his brother knew exactly what he was about to say.

"Her name is Eleanor," he answered. "And she lives in America."

CHAPTER XX

Daughter

Snow blanketed Russia when he left the country, while an unrelenting sheet of rain poured over Washington state as his plane touched down. Sergei hadn't set foot on American soil in nearly eight years. With the majority of their business interests residing in Russia and various European nations, any travel to America had been easily delegated to Dima or Pasha. He'd stayed away because an ocean between them seemed to be the only thing that could keep him from returning for Eleanor.

With no intention of staying in the country for long, he'd traveled light and after a brief exchange with a US border agent who looked overworked and sorely underpaid, he was admitted without fanfare. Swapping the SIM cards on his phone, he sent an one-line confirmation to his brothers and left the airport to meet the car that awaited him.

"Ana, are you ready yet?" Eleanor called up the stairs to her daughter as she busily plaited the last loose strands of her hair, securing the end tightly when she finished. They were preparing for the winter festival and raffle party at her school, so the whole duplex was imbued with the smell of sugar cookies and cinnamon-apple pie mixed with the scent of pine emanating from their live Christmas tree. It was the same tree they'd used for the last two years, and had been living in a large pot in the backyard between the holiday seasons. This year, she'd been forced to prune it rather aggressively to ensure that it would still fit inside their modest living room for the holiday, so it would be time to plant it come the new year.

"Ready!" Ana announced, emerging from her bedroom to appear at the top of the stairs. "Can you tie the bow for me?"

"Of course, turn the light off in your room and come down," she said. Wearing the white dress she'd brought back from Russia, with its intricate stitching and layers of exquisite fabrics, Ana looked like a proper little princess descending the stairs. She'd put on her favorite white tights that were adorned with a delicate snowflake pattern, and her little white slippers with a strap that went across each foot, secured by silver acorn buckles.

Straightening the ribbons at the waist of her dress, Eleanor tied a big fluffy bow for Ana, then encouraged her to twirl in a circle.

"Perfect!" her daughter announced with a happy cheer. After receiving the dress when her mother returned several months before, she'd promptly decided it would be the outfit she wore for the school's annual winter gala. "Now I just need my cloak," she said, seizing the door-handle to the closet in the entryway and flinging it open. Tall as she was for her age, Ana was still too small to reach the top of the closet where her cloak hung so Eleanor lifted it from the hanger and helped her daughter put it on.

"There you go," she said, securing the clasp that held it in place across her chest. "All ready now?"

"Yes!" Ana nodded enthusiastically.

"Then you take the cookies and I'll get the pie," Eleanor said, hurrying to the kitchen to collect their contributions for the buffet table. The function technically began at 6:00PM and ran until 9:30PM, but the majority of the activities were scheduled for the first two hours and it was fast approaching 7:00PM. There was fashionably late, and then there was missing out on all the fun stuff because you burnt the first batch of cookies and had to start over.

"Ready," Ana chimed from the door, platter of freshly baked and frosted cookies in hand. "Let's go!"

Eleanor grabbed the pie, flipped off the light, and rushed to catch up with Ana as she bustled through the front door and into the rain beyond. As her daughter tiptoed past the puddles to reach the car, Eleanor locked up the front door and followed her, opening the passenger door and then taking up her seat behind the wheel. Looking over her shoulder before backing out of the driveway, she looked over the dark street, searching through the shadows cast by the streetlights; she wasn't sure why, but it felt as if someone was watching her. Shaking her head, she dismissed the thought but couldn't stop the hair on the back of her neck from standing on end.

Wishful thinking, she reminded herself, flipping on the lights and backing out slowly. It'd been almost six months since she left Russia. The investigator, Mr. Kossakov, had kept in touch but reported no new information about the case. Apparently there'd been no progress on the leads she left them with, a fact that was disappointing–but there also hadn't been any further murders that they could attribute to the same killer, so that was something. In the meantime, she'd seen and heard nothing from Sergei, and she didn't feel comfortable asking the Russian investigator.

In some ways, she felt a guilty sense of relief that he hadn't followed her to America like he promised. It meant Ana was safe from whatever threats his lifestyle almost-certainly entailed, and it spared her from having to explain anything to her own mother. The ring he'd given her was safely hidden in a velvet pouch at the back of her jewelry box, not because she didn't love it and want to wear it but because she was too afraid to display it when someone was bound to ask questions.

So life was going on. Navigating toward Ana's school, she felt as though she was running on autopilot. There were a handful of Ana's teachers and some fellow parents she was loosely acquainted with because their children got along, but otherwise the event held little interest for her, especially once Ana ran off to join her friends as they engaged in musical chairs and other games for small prizes. Among the adults mingling on the sidelines, greetings were readily exchanged, holiday wishes joyfully extolled, and shallow pleasantries doled out like rice on a wedding day.

Sergei watched Eleanor leave, accompanied by a little girl dressed in the clothes he recognized. Her friend's daughter? Interesting... he reclined in his seat, waiting until her car vanished into the rainy evening. He'd been in the country for two days, just long enough to get over the worst of the jet lag and do some digging to find out where Eleanor had settled. Her previous apartment was a shit-hole near the city center but the duplex she lived in now looked decent enough. The blinds were drawn but he could see colored lights blinking through the cracks, and a string of rainbow lights had been tacked in place leading down the main walkway to the front door. Homey, if not slightly tacky and cheap by his estimation. It was vaguely reminiscent of the streets in Moscow, though there the lights were frosted white, each alight like a burning star in the freezing night. The yard was a dark slick of drowned grass and mud, with water running into the street and pooling around a drainage grate that was half-clogged with dead leaves.

Slipping around the back, he found a tiny yard that'd been turned into something of a swamp by the rain, with a covered deck that led to the back door. Forcing the lock only took a moment, then the handle clicked and the door swung open. Shaking off the excess water, he checked over his shoulder one last time before disappearing inside.

The back door led into a small kitchen that opened to an equally tiny dining area with a table and two chairs. In the living room, a Christmas tree that was heavily weighted with ornaments and strand upon strand of tinsel lit up the ground floor of the home. Strands of multicolored lights had been left on, set to blink at a slow interval, and as his eyes adjusted to the light Sergei began to see pictures and artwork on the walls.

Several posters decorated the wall space, depicting scenes of magic with mythological beasts, dragons breathing fire, and a reproduction of an old Russian painting that depicted the folk hero Dobrynya Nikitich as he engaged with an evil serpent in battle. There were framed and unframed photos, too, but few of them showed Eleanor. Instead, images of the young girl he'd seen leave the house with her that evening dominated the walls. A large, framed picture near the front door and stairs leading to the second floor, displayed a montage of pictures featuring the girl as an infant, a toddler, and in the early stages of attending school.

With a deeply uneasy feeling, he took the stairs up, two at a time but slowly so that he didn't make any noise in the process. Unless Eleanor had an unhealthy obsession with her friend's daughter...

There were three doors at the top of the stairs. The first proved to be a bathroom, of no interest to him. The second was Eleanor's bedroom, judging by the decor. At the third, he paused, hand on the doorknob, then twisted. It was a child's room alright. He leaned in the doorway, letting the door swing fully open as the reality of the situation struck him with full force.

Shades of white, pink, and gold greeted him in the low light seeping through the blinds from the streetlight outside. Beneath a plethora of stuffed animals and a patchwork quilt was a child's bed, with a bookshelf next to it already crammed full, and a small chair and desk under the window. His mind jumped back to the look on Eleanor's face when he'd caught her speaking on the phone that night. With a groan of realization, he sank into a crouched position, leaning against the wall.

He was still there when Eleanor's car pulled into the driveway two-and-a-half hours later, having returned to the living room where he'd discarded his shoes and jacket to wait, seated and silent on the small couch by their tree. The rain was still going but it'd let up to a light drizzle, and he could hear the click of her heels as she came down the walkway, accompanied by the light, little steps of her daughter. He'd looked through the kitchen for something to drink, eager to take the edge off his discomfort with the situation, but there wasn't a drop of alcohol to be found. If Eleanor did keep something in the house, it was exceptionally well-hidden.

"Go up and wash your hands, then get changed for bed," Eleanor was saying as she opened the front door and they piled through.

Sergei waited, listening as they took their shoes and coats off. The thud of small feet moved up the stairs toward the bathroom, and a moment later Eleanor stepped into the living room on a beeline for the kitchen. It only took a moment for her gaze to land on him. Freezing in her stride, he saw a look of panic cross her face and her mouth opened to scream.

He was standing in an instant, the distance between them closed in a single stride as he caught her around the waist with one arm, covering her mouth with his other hand. Recognition flashed through her eyes, and the panic gave way to shock as they heard the water turn on upstairs.

"*Tikho*," he whispered softly, easing his grip on her slightly. Eleanor nodded, and he released her mouth entirely, leaning down to steal a searing kiss before he let go entirely and sank back into a seated position on the couch.

"Mine?" he asked. He didn't need to elaborate, she knew what he meant.

"Of course," she whispered, glancing toward the stairs in apprehension. The water was still running upstairs but they didn't have much time.

"Why didn't you inform me?" he demanded.

Eleanor looked at him, a look of torment in her eyes. "Do you think I didn't want to? You have no idea how hard it was not to tell you everything."

The water shut off just then, and Eleanor froze as those tiny feet came stomping down the stairs. "Mama, can you help me out of my dress?" the girl asked as she entered the living room. A moment later, her bright blue eyes fell on Sergei with a look of inquisitive surprise.

CHAPTER XXI

Decisions

Finding out that he had a young daughter was not what Sergei had anticipated when he came to retrieve Eleanor from America. He expected a boyfriend, maybe even a husband, and was prepared to deal with the situation accordingly. Yet there he was, seated on eye level with the girl. Her hair was light blonde, almost translucent it was so pale, the same as his had been when he was very young, and she looked at him with eyes the same shade of clear sky-blue. Even without Eleanor's confirmation, he'd known from a close look at the pictures that she was his.

"*Privet,*" he greeted her, expecting a look of confusion. Instead, she looked to her mother, then back to him.

"*Zdravstvuyte,*" she greeted him in nearly-perfect Russian. There was a slight accent to her voice, but the word was otherwise crystal clear and it was his turn to look surprised as she continued. "*Menya zovut Anastasia. Vy kto?*"

"*Ti govorish po Russki?*" he asked, and she nodded affirmatively. "*Zamechatelno, molodets. Ya Sergei.*"

"She's been taking lessons for a few years now," Eleanor said by way of explanation. She looked from him to their daughter and back again, uncertainty shining in her eyes.

"Are you really Sergei?" Ana asked, taking a few small steps to stand directly in front of him.

"Of course," he answered. Regarding him with a look of intense interest, she cocked her head to the side, then reached out slowly to touch his hair.

"Then you're my father?" she asked, feeling the texture of his hair as she looked at him. After a moment, she looked over her shoulder to Eleanor, who was watching them, waiting for his reaction.

"*Da,*" he said, taking her small hand in his. "I am."

"I knew it!" she declared and, with a triumphant, childish glee, she threw herself into his arms. "I knew you'd come back someday. I've been wishing for it forever."

Taken aback, he froze at first, then wrapped his arms around her and stood, picking her up in the process. She was tall for her age but thin; she felt weightless in his arms–a billowy white cloud with platinum blonde hair braided into a crown atop her head and the color of the sky in her eyes. Eleanor stepped into the kitchen, turning on the light, while Sergei continued to study his daughter, imprinting her features indelibly upon his memory.

3:47AM

The clock was taunting her, she was certain of it. Eleanor sank onto the nearest chair and leaned over the dining room table, resting her forehead against its cool wooden surface. How could this be happening? Getting Ana to go to bed had taken forever. She still wasn't convinced her daughter would stay asleep but at least they'd managed to get downstairs without causing her to stir.

"Do you have coffee?" Sergei asked. He was standing behind her, warm hands resting on her shoulders.

"In the freezer," she answered, raising her arm halfheartedly to point in the direction of the fridge. "Milk and cream in the fridge. There's cups in the cabinet over there—" she pointed near the sink "–and sugar there. Silverware's in the top drawer. The kettle's already full so just turn the burner on high for a few minutes, and the press is on the counter."

Letting her arm fall, she lifted her head from the table and leaned back in her seat, turning her exhausted gaze in his direction. "What brings you to America?"

Sergei paused just long enough to shoot her a sardonic look. "Seriously?"

"Fine," Eleanor sighed, closing her eyes. Oh how she longed to sleep! Everything ached, from her muscles to her bones, deep and sore and tired. Stifling a yawn, she tried a different question. "How did you find us?"

"You," he said, putting all the emphasis on that word, "are not very hard to find. I had no inkling you were hiding my child or you never would have left my sight."

The tone of his voice had a sharpness to it that snapped Eleanor out of her exhausted, trancelike state. Swallowing heavily, she sat up straighter in her seat, paying closer attention to Sergei as he prepared their coffee.

"I wasn't hiding her from you," she stated. "Or do I need to remind you who up and vanished for seven years?"

"I did that for your own good," he informed her shortly. "It doesn't excuse the fact that you stayed silent in Russia."

Setting a cup down for her, he poured it nearly to the brim with the fresh, hot liquid, then added sugar and cream before presenting it to her. Eleanor accepted it with a small thanks but set the cup aside. With apprehension twisting a tight knot in her belly, she had no appetite for anything just then. Even the scent of it made her stomach turn.

"What are you going to do?" she asked once he'd taken a seat at the table. They were close enough for their knees to brush, but the proximity didn't make her heart beat with anticipation this time.

Sergei took his time about answering, sipping from his own coffee as he observed her closely. Only the light over the stove was on, casting a weak orange glow around the kitchen and dining area.

"Well?" she prompted. Sometimes she felt like an insect the way he examined her, and she didn't like it.

"*Ne znayu,*" he said, shrugging nonchalantly. "Listen, do you have anything to drink?"

"Other than coffee?" she asked, looking pointedly at their cups. Hers was still untouched, but even he hadn't drunk more than a quarter of his.

"Something alcoholic," he clarified.

"Oh, no," she answered. "You know I don't really drink. Why?"

"Just wanted something to take the edge off," he said. "*Ladno,* it's fine. I suppose seeing her father drink first thing in the morning isn't the best way to set an example."

He paused, taking another drink from his coffee. "What did you put on the birth certificate?"

Glancing him over, she sighed and pressed her lips into a thin line, rising from the table. From a shelf in the living room, she retrieved a manila envelope. Handing it to him, she sank back into her chair. Cocking an eyebrow at her, Sergei opened the envelope to remove the documents within. There were two papers. Eleanor knew them by heart. The first was Ana's birth certificate–Anastasia Sergeievna Truman, with her name listed as the mother. The second paper was a form to acknowledge paternity.

"The hospital wouldn't let me put your name on the paperwork without consent," she said. "And I didn't know your last name at the time, so–yeah."

"I see," he said, setting the papers aside. "Forgive me, Nora. If I'd known–"

"What?" she cut him off, trying to contain the derisive snort. "What would you have done, Sergei? What could you have done?"

"I would not have left you," he stated firmly, half-rising from his seat before sinking back so heavily the wood creaked under his weight. "Do you have any idea how hard it was for me? I didn't leave because I wanted to go off on some adventure. I was summoned back, informed that it was my time to rise and lead the family. You know what they had planned for me? House, wife, kids. *Vse! Ponimayesh?* My life was decided while I wasn't even present."

He paused, as though he realized he was derailing from the subject. Eleanor couldn't blame him. It was a stressful situation, tension hung thick in the air and sheer exhaustion (not to mention the jet lag she knew he must be suffering from) certainly wasn't helping either of their moods.

"Suffice to say, I would not have left you like that," he repeated, sounding weary. Lifting his cup, he looked bleakly at the contents before downing the last of the black liquid in two large drinks. "Damn it, Nora. How old it she?"

"Almost seven," she answered. Feeling slightly more relaxed, she pulled her mug closer and took a sip of the warm beverage; he'd prepared it perfectly for her. "Her birthday is the seventeenth of April."

"Why did you have her learn Russian?"

She shifted uncertainly. It was hard to tell from his tone if he was pleased or upset, or maybe just curious.

"Well, I'd say it's a work in progress," she said, trying to gauge his mood. "She started asking for lessons when she was three, and I thought it would be good for her to have part of your culture even if you were gone, so I found her a tutor. Ira's always said she picks up new words and phrases like a natural. Why?"

"Ira?" he asked.

"Her tutor," Eleanor said. "She's a really lovely woman. Grew up in Sevastopol in the eighties and then came to the US with her parents when she was nineteen. She has a wall of certifications, accolades for teaching, and Ana loves her. They have lessons twice a week."

"Indeed," Sergei said.

They were silent for a long time. It felt like somewhere between an hour and an eternity, but the next time Eleanor looked at the clock she was surprised to see that it only read 4:33AM. Only, she thought with a scoff.

"Where's your ring?" Sergei's question caught her off guard.

"Upstairs," she said, feeling guilty for having taken it off. Not that she'd entirely consented in the first place, but she had rather accepted the ring and even if she didn't admit it to him just yet, she'd grown ridiculously attached to it over the course of the previous months.

"Why aren't you wearing it?"

"Because I didn't want to explain to anyone where it came from," she answered.

"You could have simply lied," he pointed out.

Eleanor shook her head. "I'm a terrible liar."

"Uh-huh," he replied. Just two syllables, and yet so loaded.

"I didn't lie to you about Ana!" she insisted vehemently. "I'm sorry I didn't tell you, but it isn't the same thing. At all."

"On that much I will agree. Lying about my daughter is a more serious offense," he delivered the words amicably, but she knew he wasn't joking about the matter. "*Ladno*, you can put it on tomorrow." Seeing her look of hesitation, he added, "unless you no longer intend to marry me, that is."

"You say that like I ever agreed in the first place," she grumbled, folding her arms across her chest as she sank back in her seat. "Don't think I've forgotten you're a thief. For all I know, you might kill people for a living."

She'd meant the statement to be a joke of sorts but Sergei's reaction was entirely too serious for her comfort.

"I do kill people," he stated. It was cold and quiet, a simple affirmation and nothing more, but it made Eleanor shift uncomfortably in her seat when he continued. "Not for a living, mind you. That sort of work is too messy for my taste, too easy to become a slave to others."

"So you kill for revenge?" she asked.

"Sometimes," he acknowledged.

"Did you catch Olga's killer? Kossakov said there haven't been any new cases linked back to him," she said.

"*Da*," he answered. A dark look crossed his face, and Eleanor could have sworn she saw shadows in his eyes.

"Then you killed him," she surmised.

"Does that bother you?" he asked.

She shifted, avoiding his eyes. "I don't know."

"You know what he did to my sister," he said pointedly. "And all the others. Do you feel sorry for him?"

"No," she answered automatically but continued to skirt his eyes. Out of morbid curiosity, she couldn't resist asking, "who was it?"

"A criminal," Sergei answered obliquely. "Why do you care?"

Eleanor paused. Why did she care? Part of it was the fact that she felt personally invested in the matter, plus there was the fact that such a case could give one nightmares. She'd certainly had a few of those, and it was a relief to hear that he was dead, but her feelings were still mixed.

"I just hoped you wouldn't be the one to do it," she finally said.

"He was family," Sergei said. "It had to be one of us." Seeing her confusion, he clarified, "the killer was my cousin, Gleb. He was one of Yuriy's relatives, adopted into the family when his own parents died. Olga treated him like her true brother, and you know what happened to her. Still feeling sorry?"

Eleanor was horrified by the news. "I don't follow, why would he try to curse his own family?"

"Obviously he wanted us dead. He was Yuriy's sole male heir; he would have inherited practically everything." Sergei paused. "And he was a psychopath, so it doesn't matter anymore. He's dead now, it's time to move on."

It was clear from his countenance that he didn't care to discuss the topic further.

"Very well then," she said, propping her elbow on the arm of her chair in order to rest her chin in the palm of her hand. The last of her coffee was cold but she drank it anyway. "What do you intend to do now?"

Her lover regarded her seriously, considering her question at length. "That depends," he said.

"On what?" she asked.

"Whether you attempt to resist me," he said. "I'm taking you and Anastasia home with me. You will meet my brothers, and we will register our marriage."

"But we're not married," she protested.

"Aren't we?" he challenged. "A piece of paper doesn't change what already exists between us."

"And if I resist?" she asked. Sergei looked at her darkly and Eleanor felt a chill run down her spine. "Ana's already in school, she has some friends, and I have a good job. What would I tell my mother?"

"Your mother is free to visit you," he said. "I will even pay the costs."

"That's not what I meant," she said. "I mean what am I supposed to tell her about you, hm? 'Oh by the way Mom, there's one little detail I forgot to mention about Ana's dad. He's a criminal who likes to kill people'—"

"I didn't say I liked it," he cut her off, rising from his chair. When she was standing upright, the man was still several inches taller than her, but seated in her chair he positively dwarfed her. For a fraction of a second, it seemed that he might strike her as he raised his hand, and she flinched involuntarily. Tired though he had to be, Sergei caught the movement and the flash of fear that flitted through her eyes, and she saw his shoulders slump in disappointment.

"Oy, Nora," he sighed softly, completing the motion he'd begun by cupping her cheek. The pad of his thumb ran gently across her cheek and she felt her face burn red, ashamed of her reaction. "As far as your mother is concerned, I'm just another businessman. Now come, tomorrow we inform our daughter."

CHAPTER XXII

Family

To his surprise, Sergei found an unlikely ally in the form of his future mother-in-law. They met three days later, after he'd given Eleanor enough time to adjust to his arrival and accept the fact they would soon be departing the country. It'd also given him time to seriously consider the ramifications of what he was about to do.

Only Pasha, Dima, and Anton knew that he'd gone to America in order to retrieve his bride, but that wasn't the problem. The problem was Anastasia–precocious and intelligent, with eyes vibrantly alight, the sight of his daughter evoked a deeply protective, possessive feeling within him. He'd thought Eleanor was the only one capable of entangling his heart that way, of activating such a base, animalistic reaction–he'd been wrong. If anything, his feelings were stronger for Anastasia, and growing each day. She was simply so small, tiny when he compared her hands to his, with the same delicate features he recognized in Eleanor, and a fierceness of spirit that could not be rivaled. He wanted to nurture and protect her, and therein lay his conflict.

"I knew something was different when she came back from Russia," her mother was saying. They'd met at her home, a comfortable brick-built house in the suburbs, to enjoy a late lunch with just the adults while Eleanor's best friend watched Ana for a few hours.

"Call it a mother's intuition, if you will. I knew I was right when she got Ana's passport photos taken. It's not as though I'd been telling her to get it done for years, oh no. Two weeks in Russia and it's the first thing she does when she gets back, but I'm supposed to nod and believe it when she says, 'oh no, nothing special happened, it was just a normal business trip', ha!

"So–" she paused to take a long drink from her wine glass. "I'd like to hear why you left my daughter pregnant and alone all those years ago."

"Mom," Eleanor began, but Sergei gave her a nudge to be quiet.

"It's a legitimate question," he said, leaning over to kiss her lightly on the cheek. "And I'm glad your mother is so concerned for you." Turning back to her mother he continued, "I was called home by my father on an urgent business matter. I didn't know Eleanor was pregnant, or I would have certainly taken her with me. By the time things settled down, we'd lost touch.

"But this summer, we met by chance in Moscow," he continued. Most of what he said was true, or elegantly bent to fit the picture of reality that he wanted to present. He'd dressed accordingly in a silk shirt and hand-tailored suit, with a gold signet ring strategically placed over the tattoo on his hand. "After she left, naturally I had to come and convince her to marry me."

"Now that's romantic," she sighed, but then admonished him. "You should have followed her as soon as she left!"

"Mom," Eleanor hissed.

"What?" she asked. "I have a right to comment."

"I'd have liked to," Sergei said, smiling warmly as he draped an arm over Eleanor's shoulders to pull her into a sideways hug. "Unfortunately I was in the middle of an important project, and you wouldn't believe how much paperwork they make us fill out just to get a visa."

That one was a boldfaced lie, but who was keeping track? Her mother seemed to readily accept his explanations about work, and she was obviously delighted by the fact that they intended to marry. In her words, it was high time he made an honest woman of her daughter. They left lunch that afternoon on a positive note, with her mother bestowing warm hugs upon them and extracting a promise that they wouldn't get married without her.

Pasha was the only one waiting for them when the plane landed and they cleared Russian customs. His trip to the States had taken less than ten days in total, and it would have been faster if they hadn't been forced to wait several days for his daughter's visa to be approved. Looking down at Anastasia's bright-blonde head, he laid a hand on her hair and ruffled it lightly, wondering how his brothers would react to the newest addition to the family. They were expecting his bride, but he'd saved Anastasia as a surprise.

"Seryozha," his brother greeted him with a warm hug, then pivoted to address Anastasia. "And who are you, young lady?"

"Pasha," Sergei responded. Picking up Ana, he hoisted her into his arms to present her to the towering man she would call uncle. "Meet Anastasia Sergeievna Ivanova and–" he gestured to Eleanor "–Nora."

Eleanor hadn't objected in the slightest when he informed her they would be updating their daughter's documents. It was the same name she would soon have, so it only made sense that Anastasia's match. His brother's eyebrows rose at the declaration, but he nodded.

"*Khorosho,*" he agreed, extending his hand to the little girl. "*Zdravstvuyte,* Anastasia."

"This is your uncle," Sergei said, encouraging her to shake his brother's hand. "*Dyadya* Pasha. What do you think?"

"*Zdravstvuyte, dyadya* Pasha," she greeted him. Looking him over closely, she continued in carefully pronounced Russian and with a brilliant smile, "*ochen priyatno poznakomitsya.*"

"She speaks Russian?" Pasha sounded surprised and impressed. "I'm impressed, Seryozh. Where have you been hiding them?"

"*Da, ona nasha*," Sergei said, feeling a swell of pride at his brother's reaction. Pasha's acceptance was important to him, more so than perhaps anyone else.

Collecting their luggage, which was light indeed since Sergei saw little purpose in packing up half of Eleanor's household just to replace it when they were home anyway. Anything she decided she couldn't live without, he'd already assured her, she could have her mother pack up and send along. In the meantime, he could pay the rent on her duplex indefinitely or buy the damn property outright to stop her fussing about whatever else was there.

"Did you get the things I asked for?" he asked after they were settled in the car and on the way out of Moscow. Pasha nodded, glancing behind them to see Eleanor talking quietly to Anastasia in the back seat.

"Everything's been prepared," he said. "Makes more sense now, Anton and Dima were having a riot trying to guess what you wanted with a bunch of little girl's clothes and a new tea set. I think Masha has you figured, though. She went out and found a furniture set for the girl. Hasn't had it delivered yet because she wanted to be sure of her suspicions, but it's paid for and waiting."

Sergei laughed. "Oy, leave it to Masha. Tell me you were surprised, though."

"Of course," Pasha said, shaking his head when Sergei laughed some more in the side seat. "Seriously, I told Masha she was crazy when she shared her theory with me. So the girl's really yours?"

"Take another look at her and ask me that again," he suggested. "Of course she's mine. We met the first time I was there."

"Well Masha's gonna be thrilled," he said, smiling broadly. "You know how she's been on about kids lately. Maybe this'll help settle her down a bit."

Mother and daughter had fallen asleep by the time they arrived, even though it was only mid-afternoon. They'd had a long flight, and it was Anastasia's first serious trip ever so jet lag hit the girl hard. Eleanor was tired but easily roused when they arrived–their daughter was another matter.

"I knew it!" Masha crowed from the doorway when she saw the bundled-up child that Sergei carried in his arms. Realizing the girl was asleep, she immediately clapped her hands over her mouth to muffle her excited squealing as she practically hopped out the door. With an excited hug to Sergei, she bounded to Eleanor to envelop her in a huge hug.

"Welcome to Russiya," she greeted her enthusiastically, bestowing a kiss on each cheek. "I'm Maria but please call me Masha, I'm Pasha's wife. We're so happy Seryozha brought you home."

"Masha, you can talk inside. Get Brutus," Sergei said, indicating the jubilant canine who'd taken advantage of the situation to rush into the yard for a good roll in the snow. He must not have noticed the child in his arms, or Sergei knew the giant beast would have been all over her.

Taking advantage of Brutus' oversight, he hurried up the steps inside, making a beeline for his room before he'd even bothered to remove his shoes. Eleanor trailed after him, lingering close in case their daughter stirred, but Anastasia was sound asleep. Stripping her shoes and coat off, he covered her with a light blanket and left the room, dragging Eleanor out with him.

"Let her rest, she's only seven," he said. "You can join her soon, I know you're tired."

"Almost seven," she corrected him, leaning up to kiss him lightly on the lips. "Well come on then, let's help unload the car and you can introduce me to your other brothers."

CHAPTER XXIII

Marriage

"He's what?"

Lila didn't sound especially murderous to hear of Sergei's pending nuptials, but her reaction was far from one of dazzling happiness. Once again, Anton felt maligned by the gods. He was getting tired of being Sergei's errand boy for the delivery of bad news, but he couldn't resist an opportunity to visit Lila. His other excuses were few and far between.

"I didn't stutter," he stated flatly, presenting her the vase he'd just finished filling with water and the latest bouquet of flowers. "He's getting married, and he sent me to extend his personal, cordial invitation."

"When?" she asked.

"In three days," he answered. "Just long enough for his new mother-in-law to get over her fatigue and attend the ceremony."

"You must be kidding me," she sighed, sinking into her seat with a look of defeat. "When did they meet?"

"Considering the fact that they already have a young daughter, I'd say it was quite some time ago," he said. He wasn't sure why, but it brought him special pleasure to deliver that part of the news to her, though Lila didn't appear as crestfallen as he might have hoped. "Will you attend?"

"In three days?" she huffed. "Where am I supposed to find a date in that amount of time?"

"You hardly need a date," Anton pointed out. "Like it or not, you'll always be family Lila. Your father's going to attend."

Lila arched one delicate eyebrow at that news. "Oh really?"

Anton nodded. "It would seem he's satisfied with this match. And their daughter's a real cute kid, reminds him of Olga when she was little."

"Are you trying to make me cross?" she asked, glaring at him as she drummed her nails over the table.

"Of course not," he said amicably. "I just think it's time you get over your infatuation with my brother and realize there are more men in the world."

Lila looked at him critically, but after a moment something in her gaze softened and her eyes swept over him in a more appraising way. "Oh really?" she challenged. Meeting his stare, she asked him suggestively, "and are you one of those men, Anton?"

Something inside him snapped. Seizing hold of her hand, he tugged her out of her chair, knocking it to the side in order to press her back against the kitchen wall.

"Are you crazy?" she asked, each panted breath pressing her breasts against his chest. Seizing her chin, he lifted her lips to his, claiming her mouth with passionate, wild abandon.

"He's getting married in three days," he growled against her lips between kisses. "They have a daughter old enough to go to school. He doesn't need you, Lila. You're a cousin to him, a sister at best. Move on."

Whatever reaction he expected from Lila–being sworn at, struck, even bitten for daring to kiss her–the last thing he expected was for her to seize him around the neck. Pulling him tightly to her, she deepened the kiss, swirling the tip of her tongue around his in a way that made him groan hotly into her mouth. Reaching between them, she cupped his crotch through the fabric of his jeans, rubbing suggestively.

"Mm, it's about time," she panted, seizing hold of his shirt front with her other hand. "I've been waiting for your balls to finally drop for years."

Anton pulled away to stare at her. "Are you fucking serious, with the way you've treated me and all your mad obsessing over Sergei?"

"I haven't been obsessed with Sergei for years," she confessed. "A little sore about the way he treated me, wounded ego and all that, but come on. Do you really think I'm stupid enough to waste my life waiting for him?"

She laughed derisively, shaking her head of perfectly coiffed hair as she ran a hand over his chest. "You think I didn't notice how you've changed since we were kids?"

"I was never a kid around you," he disagreed.

"Teenagers are still kids in a lot of ways," she replied, leaning back to look at him seriously. "Are you really going to argue with me about this?"

He contemplated whether it was worth it, then decided to simply kiss the girl again. "If you wanted me, why didn't you ever say so?"

She shrugged, looking at him coyly. "Don't you think that's rather forward?"

He snorted. "As if that would stop you."

Lila removed her hand from its intimate position and folded her arms, frowning lightly. "Are you trying to pick a fight with me?"

"*Nyet,*" he wrapped his arms loosely over her shoulders, leaning close to nuzzle her again, eager to taste her lips once more.

"Good," she said, leaning in to kiss him. "Then we'll go together."

"Together where?" he asked, kissing along her jaw as his hands eased beneath the fabric of her shirt.

"To the wedding, idiot," she sighed, but there was no malice in her words and her breath hitched as his calloused fingertips trailed over her ribs.

They were married in what was, by Eleanor's modest standards, an extraordinarily lavish ceremony. Sergei kept insisting that it was just a small little church wedding, but with two dozen of his colleagues in attendance alongside his mother, his brothers, Masha, Dima's girlfriend Svetlana, and the rest of his extended family, she felt overwhelmed. For once in her life, the sight of her mother had proved to be a reassuring one when she arrived for the wedding, and Ana was certainly happy to see her grandmother.

"Is it always so cold here?" she'd asked as soon as she arrived. It was March, but that didn't mean much to the Russian winter that held its grip on the country firm and strong. The rest of the western world might be celebrating the beginning of spring, but not in Russia. They had two more months to go, at least!

Ana had been assigned the duties of flower girl and ring-bearer at the ceremony, two tasks that she relished and carried out joyfully. She'd spent the previous months exploring the family manor extensively in the company of the ever-devoted Brutus, learning to play chess with her uncles, and bonding with Sergei as he coached her on Russian. Soon, they promised Eleanor, they'd make her start to learn too.

The investigator from the case, Mikhail Kossakov, and his assistant Nadya, had been invited to the wedding as well. They stood in the third row, the older man's portly appearance another reassurance in an audience primarily composed of the faces of strangers. Some of the men who Sergei had invited looked like the types she'd been warned about growing up. Hardened, dangerous men with rough edges, but they were all dressed neatly in well-cut suits that must have cost a small fortune and almost everyone had a woman attending by his side. The women dressed well, extremely well, with their hair stylishly coiffed, plaited, and fluffed in all sorts of ways and jewels glittering from their ears, necks, wrists and hands. She was grateful that her mother sat at the very front, right next to Sergei's mother on one side and Masha on the other, with his brothers surrounding them. With her eyes glued to her daughter and new son-in-law, she didn't pay any attention to the questionable mix of men present as guests of the groom.

The church had been rented out for the entire day, so when the ceremony and vows were finished, the celebrants moved into the front hall to dine on a feast that'd been laid out on banquet tables during the wedding. Half a dozen waitstaff served the guests and managed the tables while the caterers continued to turn out fresh shish kebab and a variety of other meats on portable grills set up outside. Snow had been shoveled from the courtyard to make way for the grills, so the wives and girlfriends who'd attended with the men donned a variety of fur coats and gloves in order to mingle in the courtyard beyond.

"*Moya lyubimaya*," Sergei said, taking hold of Eleanor's hand. "Dance with me."

Accepting his hand, she followed him to the center of the hall where a makeshift dance floor had been established. A live group had been booked, and at a gesture from her husband–she felt her cheeks turn red just thinking the word–they began to play a traditional Russian folk song.

Soon Ana seized Dima by the hand, apologizing to his girlfriend before insisting that he take her out to dance. From the courtyard outside, Anton returned a moment later with Yuriy's youngest daughter, Lila, draped over his arm. From Sergei and Pasha's reaction when their youngest brother arrived with the girl in tow that afternoon, she'd gathered that the relationship was a new development in the family, but the young couple appeared giddy as they joined the dancing.

"Sergei," Lila called over Anton's shoulder as they danced. "*Pozdravlyayu tebya, ty svoloch.* I wish you a long and happy marriage!"

"What did she say?" Eleanor asked.

"She congratulates us," he answered. Pulling her close, he kissed her tenderly as they finished their first dance. "Perhaps I shall ask your mother to dance?"

"I think she'd love that," she answered with a nod, reaching down to gather up the skirt of her dress. It was a gorgeous creation of lace and silk, and pure white, a color Sergei insisted upon even though it was rather abundantly clear that she was no virgin when their daughter was in attendance.

Sergei handed her to Pasha for the next dance while Dima traded Ana to Anton in order to take his girlfriend to the floor, and Masha shared a friendly dance with Lila as they shared some feminine gossip, giggling between themselves. "Mrs. Truman," he said, approaching his mother-in-law, "would you honor me with the next dance?"

Smiling broadly, she set aside the glass of champagne she'd been so delicately sipping from, and accepted his hand. "Why thank you, Sergei. I would be delighted," she said, following him to the floor before resting her hand on his shoulder.

EPILOGUE

New Year

The dawning of a new year had never felt so full of promise. Standing in the warm kitchen and looking out on the Russian countryside, blanketed by a deep layer of pure white snow, Eleanor watched as Ana engaged with her father and uncles in a snowball fight fit for the history books. After several hours spent meticulously preparing for their battle like it was the second world war all over again, they were now engaged in an all-out war for total domination of the front yard. Pasha and Sergei were a team with Ana, while Dima and Anton formed the opposition.

It'd been a year since they came to Russia, returning with Sergei in a move that'd been akin to taking a plunge into arctic waters. In the span of just a few days, it felt as though the course of her life had changed forever. Eleanor didn't regret her decision, though. After a period of adjustment, life with Sergei and his extended family felt like the most natural thing in the world. It'd barely taken any time for Ana to bond with her uncles, and even Yuriy's daughter Lila liked to make an appearance from time to time, putting on the airs of an aunt to the little girl.

"Can I tell you a secret?" Masha asked. They were in the kitchen together, preparing a meal for the evening that more resembled a banquet. Beneath the table, Brutus was curled into a ball with his fluffy tail covering his nose, napping as he awaited his share of the feast. Living

164

in the same house for a year had brought the women closer together, even if that house was technically more of a manor and sometimes it felt like they each had their own apartments rather than mere separate bedrooms.

"Of course," Eleanor said, glancing over to her sister-in-law with a smile. Reaching for a damp cloth, she laid it over the dough and went to the sink to wash her hands. Judging from her glowing cheeks and the fact she'd steadfastly refused any alcohol at their new year's party the week before, Eleanor had a good idea what Masha was about to tell her.

"Don't tell Pasha yet," she said.

"I won't," Eleanor vowed, raising her hand solemnly.

"Ana will have a cousin soon," she announced with a delighted grin, placing a flour-covered hand on her belly. "I'm two-and-a-half months."

"That's wonderful!" she said enthusiastically, hugging Masha from behind. "When will you tell everyone?"

"I think Pasha already suspects something is up," she admitted, adding with a laugh, "and Brutus definitely knows. Honestly, I think that dog knew before I did. He started spending all his time following me around a few weeks ago, putting his head in my lap every time I sat down."

"There's something about animals," Eleanor agreed. Living with a dog was a new experience for her after a lifetime of no pets larger than a house cat, but she'd adapted quickly and could no longer imagine life without the great, drooling beast. Ana adored him, as one might expect of any normal seven-year-old, so much that she'd recently begun to drop very unsubtle hints about wanting a new puppy to call her very own. Maybe the prospect of a new cousin would distract her? Ha, as if. Eleanor knew her daughter wasn't so easily dissuaded. "So when will you put the poor man out of his misery?" she asked, referring to Pasha. They'd been living together long enough for her to know that if he suspected something, the curiosity would consume him until it was satisfied. Masha seemed to delight in this fact, and enjoyed stretching out little mysteries of her own design for her husband to solve.

"Oh I'll tell him," she assured Eleanor with a hearty laugh. "Probably tonight now that I've told you, otherwise he'll read you like an open book and there won't be any chance of surprising him."

"That's not fair," Eleanor protested. "I can keep a secret."

"Not really," Masha laughed, shaking her head.

"Hmph," she snorted. "Tell that to Sergei. I kept a whole daughter secret." She stuck her tongue out at Masha in childish triumph.

"That hardly counts. He found out as soon as he returned to your country," Masha countered. "It's okay, we love you even if you're terrible at keeping secrets."

A thud against the window jolted their attention back to the great war of snowballs being waged in the yard. From the look of it, Anton and Dima were getting pelted into submission by Ana as she perched high atop Pasha's shoulders. Her normally pale cheeks and nose were bright pink from the cold, a wild grin on her face as she laughed and flung snowballs at her cowering uncles like a little blonde maniac on a quest for world domination. Sergei was laughing too, marching theatrically around in the snow as he kept their daughter readily supplied with a flow of fresh snowballs.

"They'll be done soon, and then they'll bring all that lovely snow inside to melt on the floor," Masha sighed, shaking her head at the men behaving like children. Soon all of them were flopping about in the unspoiled patches of snow that remained, stretching their limbs out to make figures in the powder.

"It's alright," Eleanor said, grinning at Ana as she came up to the glass to stand on tiptoes, peering into the kitchen. "I've prepared the *banya* for them, so they can just strip off and head in there. The pie should be finished cooling by the time they're done."

As predicted, the five snow-covered warriors soon completed their war games with Ana leading a victorious march into the front entry. Pasha had fashioned a fake gun for her out of some spare wood that was lying around, and she pointed it at her captive uncles, forcing them to march into the kitchen with their hands behind their back.

"*Privet* Mama, cadet Ivanova reporting from battle," she announced, planting her feet firmly together at the heels and saluting the way her father and Dima had taught her. "We have obliterated the enemy fortifications and taken them captive. I now present them as substitutes to do my chores."

She smiled hopefully, batting her little eyes at her mother in the hope that her ruse would succeed.

"You obliterated them, huh?" she asked, looking first at Ana as she nodded vigorously, and then over her head to raise an eyebrow at Sergei. "I see. And now you'd like to sentence them to hard labor?"

"*Da!*" the little girl proclaimed. "Why? Because, Mama, *eto zakon voyni.*"

"The law of war," Sergei translated helpfully.

"What do you think, prisoners?" she asked, looking to Dima and Anton skeptically as Brutus emerged from beneath the table to greet the family.

"Oh saintly one, *ya umalyayu*–take pity upon us," Anton said, falling on the kitchen floor theatrically at her feet. Brutus used the opportunity to enthusiastically disperse slobbery kisses all over his face, only stopping when Anton gently shoved his head away. "Please, not the gulag!"

"Have no mercy!" Masha cried from her position at the stove, making a show of shaking her fist at them. "Someone must clean the floors, look at the mess they've made!"

All five glanced at their feet, taking notice of the trail they'd left across the floor and then sharing a guilty look between them.

"Oh don't worry about it," Eleanor said, shaking her head and laughing at their antics. "Away with the lot of you!" Taking Ana's mock-gun, she shooed them out of the kitchen. "The *banya* is ready and waiting for you, go and get warm, get clean. Then come back and enjoy some pie, but be quick–" she gave them a sly look "–you never know when Brutus will strike!"

If the Russian winter was cold during the day, it was downright frigid at night. Temperatures had sunk into the subzero range, arctic-level cold that turned water to ice as you watched, and kept most sane people bundled up inside the warmth of their homes. Eleanor would have been inside too, except that the serene calm of the night had lured her into the back garden. They were only going to spend one more day at the dacha before returning to their Moscow residence, so she wanted to enjoy the unpolluted night one last time. Stars lit the sky up even though the moon was nowhere to be seen, working in concert with the unbroken blanket of snow that stretched to the horizon in order to light the night up almost like early morning. Fortunately, the fur-lined coat that Sergei had insisted she keep for winter use proved impenetrable to the cold, so between her boots combined with her gloves and hat, only the front of her face felt any hint of the chill.

Behind her, the snow crunched as her husband approached. A year on and she was finally used to the term. It'd taken time to wear it in, almost like a new pair of shoes, but now it felt comfortable, familiar. And she was his wife.

"I hear the family is expecting a new addition," he said, stopping just behind her to stand still and look up at the sky with her.

"And Masha claims I can't keep a secret," she scoffed, half-turning to look at Sergei and grin. "She's told Pasha then?"

"Da," he nodded. "When did you find out?"

"This afternoon," she said, leaning up to give him a kiss. "I suppose we'll tell Ana in the morning?"

He nodded. "I tucked her in with Brutus, so I'm sure they're asleep."

"Dima was in an awful rush to get out of here earlier," she commented, leaning back into his arms. "Where was he off to?"

"Sveta called," he answered. His breath warmed the back of her ear as he spoke, using the tip of his nose to nuzzle along her hairline.

"Do you think they'll get married this year?" she asked.

"They might," he said. "Her father's a prosecutor, so she wants Dima to be squeaky clean before they meet. We'll see."

"Indeed," she agreed, sighing softly. His tone told her it would be a cold day in hell before Dima could be deemed 'squeaky clean' but she wasn't going to ask for all the details. She'd learned over the course of the previous year that there were some things Sergei preferred not to discuss with her. And some things meant anything to do with the shadow deals they handled on the side, including the sporadic business trips they took every few months to Europe. Masha advised her to watch a soap opera and pick up a hobby to stay busy during those trips, because the anticipation waiting for their return could wreck her mental health. So far she'd abided by those methods, or spent the time staying busy with Ana, but soon her need to know would win out.

"Come inside," he entreated her, turning her around to see her face in the silver-white light of the stars. "The fire's still alive, the child sleeps. Dima is gone, and Pasha and Masha have their own happiness to celebrate."

"Why, Mr. Ivanov," she admonished him lightly, pulling back as he leaned forward to kiss her. "It sounds very much as though you're trying to seduce me."

"Never," he said mock-seriously. "If I were trying to do that, I would tell you I've poured out two glasses of your favorite champagne."

"Oh I see," she stepped backward through the snow, slow and deliberate with her eyes on Sergei as he followed, holding on to her gloved hands. "And of course you haven't procured any of those sinfully delicious bourbon cherries..."

"Certainly not," he stated in agreement, making a stern face of rejection as he shook his head. "Nor will you find a trail of rose petals leading to our bed."

As they spoke, he backed her toward the door to the kitchen, and finally Eleanor turned with a laugh, tugging the screen door open. She preceded Sergei into the kitchen, laughing softly as he shushed her.

"Be quiet, you'll wake up the little tyrant," he warned, tugging her into his arms to silence her with a kiss.

"Oh really?" she whispered teasingly. "She's a little tyrant now, is she?"

"Did I say tyrant?" he asked, letting her go so they could divest themselves of their boots and jackets. "I meant our darling, angelic child."

"Ah, but of course," she said.

Stripped down to their regular clothes, they continued through the kitchen to the living room. True to his word, the fire was crackling away happily, fulfilling its duty in keeping the cold at bay. Sergei fetched their champagne, handing her the glass and raising his own for a toast.

"To you, my most darling, beloved woman," he said. "One year ago you came here, almost without question, to join me in my homeland. You have given me a daughter, and brought completion to my family. *Ya lyublyu tebya*, Eleanor."

More from Victoria Wright

The Lvov Family

Dukes, Duels & Daring - Book I

Lords, Love & Liberty - Book II *(Coming 2018)*

Sons of the Motherland

Sergei - Book I

Ruslan - Book II

Vitaliy - Book III *(Coming 2018)*

Dmitri - Book IV *(Coming 2018)*

Nikolai - Book V *(Coming 2018)*

Intruder

There were certain things in her life that Vivian was certain she would never forget. The loss of her first tooth was one, a memory forever tied to the taste of her own blood. Burying her beloved cat at the age of nine was another, the first time she'd ever lost a loved one to the cold embrace of death. Then there was Carlo's call some two months ago—she would always remember how her brother's voice sounded that day. He'd been shaken, for the first time that she could ever recall, serious and grave as he informed her that their parents were in the hospital, that their father's life hung in the balance.

Above and beyond all else, she would never forget the night *he* came, hell bent on destroying her life forever.

Ruslan.

She didn't know his last name. According to him, she didn't need to. Like a storm fresh off the ocean, he swept her away with all the violence of a hurricane. Except that he was worse than a hurricane, because at least with a hurricane you knew it was going to end, that everything would recover and someday life would go back to being normal. Glaring at the back of her captor's dark-haired head, she could only guess at how long her imprisonment would last.

Three Days Earlier

It was raining, pouring down in huge, heavy droplets that drummed over the roof and trees before making their way to the sodden earth below. Usually the sound of rain would have been soothing, but no matter how hard she tried, Vivian just couldn't relax. She'd been wound up all day, a feeling of tension that coiled through her, keeping her on edge. She couldn't shake the sense that someone was watching her—and it wasn't Franco or Luca because they'd been watching her ever since the botched hit on her father.

"Earth to Miss V, do you read me?" the sound of Luca's voice jolted her out of her thoughts. Turning her attention to him, she glared at the man who'd been tasked with babysitting her, patently unamused by his attempt at humor.

"What?" she demanded testily.

"Hey now, no need to bite my head off," he said, raising his hands defensively. "You've been a mile away all day, we just wanted to know if you need anything—Franco's gonna make a run over to the shop for some cheese and crackers."

Vivian shrugged, gazing back toward the window and the darkening sky beyond. "I don't know, just get me something to drink."

"You wanna be a little more specific?" Luca asked. "Whaddya want, some orange juice or something?"

"What, am I twelve?" she returned, rolling her eyes. "Tell him to pick me up a bottle of booze, vodka or rum but make sure it's the good stuff."

"You want something to eat with that, or you just plan on spending the night puking it up when you're done?" he asked, evidently unfazed by her request.

"Oh ha, ha, ha, you're so funny." If she didn't sound amused, it was because she wasn't. The whole babysitting thing had gotten old within the first week, never mind almost two months of being watched over like she was made of porcelain. If she'd wanted the constant companionship of her father's goon squad, she would've stayed at home on the East

Coast instead of returning to complete her studies in Washington. She knew her father meant well when he sent Luca and Franco to keep an eye on her—he was understandably on edge after almost being killed—but for two men in their thirties, the pair could be remarkably immature and downright annoying at times. The only thing they seemed to take seriously was their job, and that meant she'd barely had two seconds to herself since they'd been assigned to guarding her. For God's sake, she'd had to fight them for the right to use the bathroom unattended!

"Well, is that a yes or no on the food part?" Luca was still watching her expectantly, waiting for her to answer his question.

"Fine, get me a pizza, pepperoni with stuffed crust and none of those disgusting toppings you two like," she sighed.

"Sure thing, you want that fresh or frozen?"

"Oh for fuck's sake Luca, I don't care!" she snapped, slamming her fist against the table. "It's pizza and liquor, what is so hard about that? It's not like I asked for a five-course dinner or said he should go to Italy to get it."

Her guardian let out a low whistle, shaking his head. "Jeez Louise, Miss V, you ain't gotta scream at me over it." Through the open door, he called down the stairs to Franco, "Her Royal Highness wants a pizza and some booze, make it rum or vodka and don't cheap out!"

"What kinda pizza?" Franco's voice carried up the stairs.

"One of those stuffed crust ones with pepperoni and nothin' else," Luca answered, "and grab me some lasagna or something, will ya?"

"You got it," Franco confirmed, followed by the heavy oak door banging shut behind him as he left.

Vivian could only shake her head—where did her father even find guys like Franco and Luca, some factory out east where they spit out mafia-wannabes like candy from a Pez dispenser? Sighing, she opened the lid of her laptop and reached for her headphones, intent on finding some distraction from her feelings of uneasiness and Luca's intermittent snickering as he watched the latest episode of another brainless car show. No sooner had she done so, her phone buzzed on the table. Picking it up, she was greeted by a message from Heather, one of the roommates she'd had before having to take a place by herself in order to accommodate Luca and Franco's newfound presence in her previously peaceful, almost-normal life.

'do u have a d8 for homecoming?'

Ha, that's a good one. Heather knew she wasn't a fan of dating, mostly because the guys they knew were dumbass idiots who drank too much, partied too hard, and pretty much just wanted to get up every skirt they saw when they weren't figuring out how to cheat their way past the next test or bribe someone into writing their term papers. Not that Heather seemed to mind the sex part, given her propensity for going through guys like some girls went through shoes. Use 'em or lose 'em was her motto, and one she certainly lived by. But there was another reason for Vivian's reluctance to engage with the so-called eligible bachelors they went to school with, and it went by the name Daddy.

'Don't think I'll go this year,' she responded, fingertips flying over her screen with practiced ease.

Heather's response was nearly instant. 'y not?!?!?!?! u no I need u there 2 make sure I don't do something stupid'

As if that was even possible. Stubborn as an ox would've been a nice way of putting it—fact was, Heather basically did whatever she wanted, whenever she wanted. Sometimes Vivian actually wondered how she managed to maintain a nearly perfect GPA without sleeping with her teachers, but truth was the girl had a mind like a steel trap if she cared enough to remember something, and she was surprisingly passionate about her studies.

'Sorry, you're gonna have to drag someone else along this time. Maybe Kristy or Lauren? I bet they're gonna go.'

'no way, K's turned in2 a total bitch and have u seen L's new haircut?! u have 2 go, I found a gr8 guy 4 u!'

Of course, for someone capable of pulling straight-As at one of the country's leading universities, the fact Heather didn't give a shit about spelling things properly in text messages was something Vivian would never understand.

'For the love of God, could you at least *try* to spell properly? You're making my eyes bleed.'

'will u go 2 the dance if I do?'

Glancing over to Luca, she weighed her options. With or without a date, she usually didn't mind attending various social functions just for the hell of it (and maybe for the free booze, too) but there was no way in hell she'd attend with her resident babysitters trailing along. And since there was no sign of them leaving anytime soon, she'd resigned herself to a lack of socializing for the foreseeable future.

'I'll think about it, so make your English teachers proud now. Who's the guy, you got a picture?' Curiosity might've killed the cat, but satisfaction brought it back. Even if she wasn't going to date him, she couldn't help wanting to know who Heather had managed to dig up.

'Great! You better be thinking about what you'll wear because no way am I gonna accept no for an answer. His name's Nick and I swear he's NOT a geek, a loser, or a frat boy. Whaddya think, hot as hell right?' Her message was accompanied by three pictures of a clean-cut young man with dark eyes, light-brown hair, and a lithe torso with just the right amount of muscle. If she was being honest, he actually looked pretty good. Maybe not hot as hell, as Heather put it, but then she'd always been slightly more cerebral—she needed more than a handsome face or ripped body to like a guy, she had to know that there was something going on inside his head too.

'Brains before brawn, you know me. Where'd you find him, and what's he studying? I assume he's still a student if you're talking about homecoming...'

The doorbell rang just then, making her jump in surprise, and her eyes flew from her phone to Luca as he grabbed the remote and shut the TV off. It was too soon for Franco to be back, and they weren't expecting any visitors. Hell, Vivian's own friends didn't know where her new place was because her father was just paranoid enough that he wanted it kept on the down-low for security.

"You expecting someone?" Luca asked quietly, glancing to her over his shoulder. He'd already grabbed his gun from the side table, his entire demeanor shifted from relaxed to dead serious in the span of a second.

"No one," she breathed, feeling her stomach twist as her heart hammered hard against her ribs. "Maybe it's the neighbors?"

"Yeah, maybe," he didn't sound convinced. "Go to your room and stay quiet."

Usually she would have balked at being treated like she was five, but her instincts said to obey. Leaving her laptop on the table, she reflexively pocketed her phone and hurried to her room, cringing when the door creaked as she opened it. Luca motioned for her to close the door so she obeyed, frightened gaze lingering on him until it clicked shut. A moment later, she heard the stairs sigh and groan as he descended toward the front door. The doorbell rang again, just once, followed by a silence that frightened her more than anything. Pressing her ear to the door, she strained to hear Luca's voice, praying that it was just a neighbor in need of something mundane like a couple of eggs or a bag of sugar—neighbors still borrowed things like that, right?—or even someone who had the wrong house number. Half the houses on the block looked the same, after all, plus it was pouring rain and getting dark outside. It would've been easy for someone to get mixed up, sometimes even she pulled into the wrong driveway!

So why was every hair from the back of her neck to her ankles standing straight up? As much as she might try to hide it, she was still the daughter of a mafia man, and right then every drop of that mafia blood screamed danger. Hearing the stairs again, she cracked her door open a hair's breadth, hoping beyond hope to see Luca come back into the room with one of those goofy, lopsided smiles on his face that said everything was okay.

Instead, the dark-clad figure of a man entered the room, handgun with a silencer held at his side and a balaclava concealing his face. Vivian's blood ran cold, hand frozen on the knob, as the intruder's gaze moved straight to her door. His eyes fixed on hers, and for a moment she was certain he would raise the gun to fire on her. Instead, he crossed the room in three long strides and came to a full stop right in front of her.

"Knock-knock, Vivian." His voice was soft, his English accented, and horror coursed through her as adrenaline rushed hot in her veins. Why did she have to take a bedroom on the second floor? For a split second, she considered rushing to the window and jumping out, but with nothing save for a concrete patio to soften the fifteen-foot fall, she'd be lucky not to break her legs in the process.

"Oh fuck."

In the next moment, she was knocked back by the force with which the intruder entered her room, slamming the door open so hard the knob was embedded in the wall. Scrambling backwards, she tried to rise back onto her feet only for the masked man to descend on her. Straddling her waist, his weight alone was enough to pin her to the floor as he holstered the gun beneath his jacket.

"Luca!" she screamed, lifting her arms in a futile attempt to resist. "Help!"

"Luca is bleeding out in the hall," the man informed her, catching her wrists roughly and pinning them to the floor with one hand. With the other hand, he withdrew a syringe from another pocket. Her eyes widened, searching desperately for an escape as she struggled against his iron grip. "Shh, this won't hurt if you hold still."

"Like hell I will—help, someone help!" She tried twisting away but it was an effort in vain. In one smooth motion, he popped the cap off the syringe and jabbed her at the junction of her neck and shoulder, just above the collarbone. She opened her mouth to scream for help again, only to be silenced by the masked man as he clapped a gloved hand tight across her lips. Acting automatically, she sank her teeth into his hand, biting as hard as she could and tasting leather in the process—but her assailant was unfazed and his grip didn't so much as loosen, though she could have sworn she saw his deep-blue eyes flash with pain as his face hovered close over hers.

"*Tikho*," he growled, maintaining his hold on her wrists no matter how hard she struggled and tried to twist free. "*Spi sladko.*"

Whatever else the attacker may have said was lost to the blackness that consumed her vision then. The last thought that crossed her mind before it was claimed by dark oblivion was, *fucking hell, why didn't I get a gun like Daddy told me to?*

Printed in Great Britain
by Amazon